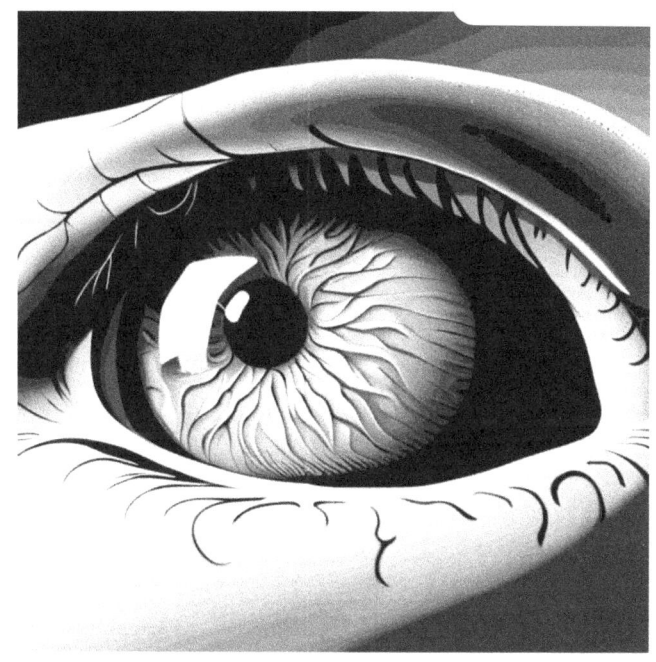

# Draconim Lacrima Mortis
## *Tear of The Dragon*

A contemporary eco-fantasy
By
Lawrence Nault

# *Get Your Copy Today*

# DIVERSION

## A MacIver Kids Adventure

*By*
**Lawrence Nault**

ISBN 978-1-7380681-3-5

# Prelude

The spacecraft entered Jupiter's atmosphere just south of the planet's equator. Traveling at 108,000 miles per hour, this was not a controlled descent, but a suicide dive into the Jovian atmosphere. It was 2:57 p.m. on September 21, 2003, when NASA directed the Galileo into Jupiter, knowing that the speed and friction would tear apart the spacecraft and the pieces would vaporize before they made it far into the planet's gaseous atmosphere.

"It has been a fabulous mission for planetary science, and it is hard to see it come to the end," commented one of the mission's project managers.

It wasn't an accident. It was intentional. A planned destruction engineered to prevent the spacecraft from crashing into Europa, one of the moons of Jupiter, and possibly contaminating an ocean hidden under the ice. A project that cost 1.4 billion dollars, involved 100 scientists and close to 800 people, and lasted almost 14 years, was intentionally terminated in a ball of flames.

This is the story we were told…

_____

October 12, 1989, was the scheduled launch for the 31st space shuttle mission, the 5th flight of the space shuttle Atlantis.  STS-34 did not take off. A faulty main engine controller on main engine number two resulted in the launch being delayed. They tried again on October 17th but poor weather at the emergency landing site, the Kennedy Space Center, led to the launch being scrubbed once again.  On October 18, at 12:53:40 EDT, after a short delay to update the onboard computer and carrying the Galileo/Jupiter spacecraft as its primary payload, the Space Shuttle Atlantis launched itself into the skies over the Kennedy Space Center.

The flight of Atlantis was almost aborted three times as it orbited Earth because of malfunctions. Had it not been for the nuclear device powering their payload and the fear of causing an international incident, it probably would have been aborted. With only a six-second window to deploy the Galileo spacecraft, the spacecraft was successfully deployed at 18:15 EDT, six hours after launch. Using the IUS booster, Galileo was injected into a Venus transfer orbit before it separated from its booster.

The booster was not enough to carry Galileo to its final destination.  Gathering that speed required a triple gravity assist from Venus, Earth, and Earth again, to develop enough momentum to carry it to Jupiter. Twenty feet tall and weighing almost 6,000 pounds, the spacecraft consisting of an orbiter and an entry probe, Galileo hurtled towards Venus traveling at 9,000 miles per hour on the first phase of its five-year mission. It would slingshot around Venus, then twice around Earth before making its way to Jupiter, where it arrived on December 7th, 1995, a six-year journey.

On December 16th, 1997, at 4:49 a.m., just after Galileo's primary mission had concluded, a signal was received back at Earth telling scientists that the Galileo had passed just 124 miles above Europa. Scientists received information about more images documenting the surface of Europa to add to the 1,800 images received during Galileo's primary mission. They were able to identify what they thought was some of the most recent geological activity on the moon and areas where the ice crust had broken open and been filled by some darker material.

The mission was a resounding success. What was originally a twenty-three-month mission with an 11-orbit tour and 10 close encounters of Jupiter's major moons was extended three times resulting in 35 close passes in total. Eleven of these close encounters were with Europa, eighter were with Callisto, eight with Ganymede, seven with Io, and one with Amalthea. It provided data and images that stimulated additional study of Jupiter for decades, but in particular Europa which they identified as "one of the most promising places where we might find currently habitable environments in our solar system." A one-hundred-mile-deep saltwater ocean covered with a twelve-mile-thick icy crust, heated by the moon's core from vents on the ocean floor.

Europa quickly became one of the scientific community's top priorities and in 2015 NASA formerly gave the greenlight to the Europa Clipper mission which will launch in 2024 and arrive at Jupiter in 2030. The mission includes 50 flybys of the Jupiter moon, with some as close as

16 miles from the surface as they not only study the moon but also search for a potential landing area for the lander mission not far behind it.

That's the official news and reports that have been provided to the public on the Galileo mission and Europa.

The failure of the molybdenum-mesh high gain antenna to deploy was well documented. News stories described how they attempted to free up seemingly seized components of the arm by hammering at it using a motor turning off and on 180 times in 2 ½ minutes. They blamed the problem on three composite ribs stuck in the folded position and even concluded that their attempted fix increased pressure on the jammed parts.

December 16th, 1997 was not just the day that the Galileo made its closest pass to Europa though. It was the day two of the three jammed ribs finally gave way to the pressure they were under and broke free from the spacecraft. It is entirely possible that the engineers at NASA's Jep Propulsion Laboratory never knew as they had long since abandoned the process of trying to get the high-gain antenna opened. Even if their telemetry did tell them that pieces had fallen off their spacecraft, it is well within reason that they would expect those pieces to just become space debris. Even if that debris fell into a decaying orbit, it would only make sense that it would burn up as it fell into the atmosphere. That is what would be expected…

2.8 billion miles, 14 years, 34 orbits of Jupiter, 3 mission extensions, 2 asteroid flybys, 1.4 billion dollars, and to prevent forward contamination NASA did the responsible thing and destroyed their spacecraft when they knew they would no longer be able to communicate with it and control it. To prevent forward contamination….

# Chapter 1

It was a madhouse at the MacIver's. For the first time since they had moved to Canada Will and Janet, the MacIver kids' parents, were traveling back to Scotland for a much-needed vacation, and to re-unite with family. They had intended to delay the trip a couple more years, but Janet's mother was having some health issues and her brother suggested that it might be a good idea to return home sooner. This change of plans unfortunately meant that they could not take the kids to Scotland with them. Traveling overseas with 10 kids wasn't something easily accomplished on short notice. The trip on short notice, combined with the stress of Janet's mother being unwell, was stressful enough, but this was also the first time they traveled anywhere for more than a couple of days without any of the kids.

Amar's grandparents sat in the living room and observed the commotion in the house. His grandfather didn't move around much anymore. He was only out of the hospital for a few months since his incident with the Loma, and his recovery was slow. Amar sat with his grandparents, drinking chai, and keeping them company. Janet came in and the stress was showing on her face.

"I can't thank you enough for offering to stay with the kids on such short notice," Janet said as she watched Brad and her husband carry the luggage out the door.

"If you need anything I put all the contact information up on the fridge door, and all the kids have a copy of it in their phone."

"We will be fine Mom," said Allen as he rolled into the room with Fritter at his side.

"We stocked up the fridge and pantry and the freezer in the basement. I e-transferred you some money in case you need to buy more groceries or anything else. Have I missed anything?" asked Janet.

"Car is loaded, Hun," said Will as he came back into the house with Brad. "We don't want to be late getting to the airport and who knows what traffic will be like when we get near Toronto."

"Let me go find the kids and say good-bye," said Janet.

Before she could move Brad's voice boomed through the house. "MacIvers line up for inspection!"

Brad's mother gave him a wry look while his father just laughed. It sounded like a stampede in the house as all of the kids raced from their various locations in the house to the living room. Janet started to say good-bye but ended up choking back tears. Antonia gave her a hug.

"Have a good trip, Mom, and tell Grandma I hope she is feeling better soon,"

One by one, each of the MacIver kids gave their mother and father a hug and wished them a good trip.

"If there is anything you need," Janet started, but Amar's grandfather interrupted her.

"Go, go. This old man is tired and needs some peace and quiet," he said in a half-hearted grumpy tone as he winked at Will who was standing by the front door.

Reluctantly Jill went quiet and made her way to the car. Some of the kids followed to watch them drive off, standing in the street and waving with exaggerated motions as their parent's car headed down the road.

Back in the house, Amar's Grandmother was already in the kitchen, setting out the sweets she had brought over. The kids gathered around the table and dug into the treats as they talked about their plans while their parents were away. It was also the first time many of them had spent any time with Amar's Grandfather since he had been in the hospital. He had been in a coma for almost 4 months and then spent another month in the hospital before the doctors would release him to go home. In the three months since he had made a fair recovery, but he still wasn't the same man he was before the incident with the Loma.

"Don't you young'uns be making any crazy plans just cause your parents are gone. I may not move fast, but you gotta come home sometime."

The kids laughed.

"I am glad you are, Grandpa," said Kelly. "We haven't seen you in a long time."

"Don't be getting ideas," Amar's grandmother spoke up. "He isn't hiking into the hills or chasing down anything as long as I have a say."

Amar's Grandfather slipped a folded-up paper onto the table. Bjorn recognized it immediately and smiled. Sheila reached out and unfolded the paper, revealing the drawing that Bjorn had made of the spaceship with the phrase "Our destiny awaits. Join us," written on the bottom. She passed the paper to Deane, her twin, and it worked its way around the table.

"I want you to know that I always knew when you guys were at the hospital, and I know your parents asked you not to bother me while I was healing up, so it is okay that you didn't come by the house."

Amar's grandfather stopped to catch a breath.

"That drawing Bjorn, was the first thing I saw when I woke up. I have kept it with me every day since. Thank you! And yes, I will join you."

Bjorn smiled shyly, slightly embarrassed.

"Well, they left almost a year ago, so hopefully that is all done and over with," said Brad. "Still not sure it really happened some days."

Amar's Grandfather smiled and looked over to Allen who looked back at him knowingly. The conversation was interrupted by Amar's Grandmother who asked for some help clearing the table as she put a tray of hot naan bread down in the center of the table. The food that followed the naan bread was amazing, and there was always something on the kitchen table to eat throughout the rest of the day, which the MacIver kids took full advantage of as they came and went throughout the day.

It was a typical day for the MacIvers, aside from their parents being gone and Amar's grandparents being at the house. Everyone did their own thing. Hanging out in the tree house. In their rooms reading, listening to music, casually scrolling through YouTube videos, and drawing. Some of them off playing sports. Brad spent a good part of his day in the driveway working on a small motorbike he had just bought for himself. He got it cheap because it wasn't running, which is also why he didn't get much of an objection from his parents. Brad was confident that he could get it going though.

"Hey," Amar's grandmother said in a startled voice as she jumped a little at the feel of Fritter's wet tongue on her leg.

"Sorry," Allen said. "Never have been able to break her from that habit."

Amar's grandmother set down her chai on the patio table and reached down to pet Fritter who promptly made her way into her lap. Allen moved to get Fritter down, but Amar's grandmother motioned that he didn't need to, as she sat back in her chair and looked out to the driveway. Her husband was on the ground, tools in hand, helping Brad work on the motorcycle.

"Keeping an eye on Baba?"

Amar's grandmother looked at Allen curiously and raised an eyebrow.

"Amar taught me. I hope that is okay for me to call him that."

"He would like that very much, Allen. So do I. You kids are our family."

They both watched the work taking place on the motor bike.

"He seems to be doing much better."

"He has not moved this much in many, many months. You guys are good for him." Amar's grandmother paused, looking off into the distance as she pet the basset hound in her lap. "Did you know when we were young, Baba, which I hope you all start calling him, and yes you kids should call me Nani. Did you know he used to drive me everywhere on the back of his motorcycle? He drove like a madman."

"Maybe he can give you a ride on Brad's motorbike when they get it running," said Allen.

Nani shooed Fritter off her lap and stood up, grabbing her near-empty coffee cup to head into the house. She looked down at Allen with a seemingly stern look on her face.

"If Brad even thinks about letting that old man sit on that motorcycle I will flatten the tires myself."

Allen broke out in laughter, and Nani smiled back at him as she started to walk towards the door.

"He talks, sometimes in his sleep, sometimes just to tell me."

Allen spun his wheelchair around so he could face Nani.

"It's not over for him. He says they will be back Allen."

Allen could see the concern and worry on Nani's face. He thought a moment or two before responding.

"It was scary for all of us, and we all worried when he was in hospital. It might seem like he is still scared and that is why he says that, but I don't think that is it. I think he knows, like I do, that there is more to come."

Amar's grandmother stood quietly, looking out at her husband in the driveway, listening to the excitement in his voice as he helped Brad. She bent down and gave Allen a hug and a kiss on the cheek.

"I know. Keep him safe please."

Allen nodded and Nani returned to the house and back into the kitchen which seemed to be her happy place, where she started to prepare even more food.

"We are all going to have to join Kelly on her runs if she keeps making food like that."

Allen spun around to find Antonia behind him.

"Something you should be telling us, Allen?  I was sitting around the corner and kind of overheard."

"Just a feeling…"

The conversation was interrupted by the phone sitting on the patio table ringing. Nani must have forgotten it there. Antonia picked it up, saw her mother's name on the screen, and answered it.

Allen listened to the conversation, giving his sister they side-eye look when he heard her tell her mother that she was the only one home and everyone was off doing their own thing and Amar's grandparents were napping.

"I will let everyone know you got there safe and are getting on the plane.  Have a safe trip, Mom.  Love you."

Antonia hung up the phone and looked at her brother.

"You know as well as I do that Mom would have waited to talk to every one of us.  Probably would have missed her plane doing that.  I could feel Dad stressing behind her," said Antonia.

Allen nodded as Nani poked her head out the door. Antonia handed her the phone.

"Did I hear it ring?" asked Nani.

"Mom called," replied Antonia. "I told her you guys were napping and everyone was off doing their own thing."

Nani smiled at Antonia and tapped her temple.

"Smart girl. Call everyone in for supper, and make sure you tell those two to get out of their filthy clothes and clean the grease off their hands before coming into my kitchen."

Allen and Antonia headed off to round everyone up. It took a while, but eventually everyone found their way to the kitchen and their place at the table.

"Who ordered in Indian," said Amar as he walked into the kitchen. He was surprised by the smack of a spatula on his backside.

"Sit your butt down," Nani ordered. She placed a last dish of food on the table before sitting down herself.

"It is nice to have family around the table. I won't be cooking like this every day, but I will always have something ready you can help yourself to. Your Mom and Dad are on the plane now. I know you are all good kids, but your parents' rules are my rules, so please remember that. And you, mister," Nani said as she pointed at Brad. "I am giving you fair warning. If you let that feeble old man even close to sitting on your motorcycle I will flatten the tires, and I will put sugar in the gas tank! Understood?"

"I can drive a motorbike," said Baba.

"You drive like a madman, and you are 100 years old," replied Nani. "One more thing," she added and paused to wait for the giggles to die down. "There is no Mr. or Mrs. here. Nani, "she said as she pointed at herself, "and Baba" she added as she pointed at her husband. "Now eat."

They didn't have to be asked twice. The MacIvers dug into the food on the table and supper was a noisy commotion of conversation and cutlery clattering against plates. Baba regaled the children with tales of his motorcycle days, ignoring the looks from his wife across the table. When they had all eaten until they were full, Nani watched as the kids worked together to clean off the table, wash the dishes, and clean the kitchen. She was impressed.

"Why is Fritter barking like that?" asked Joane as she looked out the kitchen window.

Allen made his way over to the window to see what was going on as Fritter's barking became the howl that only a hound dog could make. Allen tried calling Fritter in, but Fritter didn't move or stop her howling, which was very unusual. It took Allen going out to the yard and putting a hand on Fritter for her to quiet down. Allen could feel her vibrating. He looked around to see what she was seeing, but there was nothing. Dawn and Brad came out to see what was going on and Baba soon joined them. Dawn got down on the ground and pulled Fritter into her lap, holding the shivering dog.

"Everything okay?" asked Brad.

"I have no idea what is stressing her," replied Allen.

Brad looked around and tried to follow the direction Fritter was looking in, but he didn't see anything either.

"You kids ate a lot of food at supper. You should probably walk some of it off," said Baba. "A walk might help your dog too," he added before making his way back to the house.

"Well, that was random," said Dawn.

Allen looked out towards the trails and where what was once hills was now a valley.

"Maybe not," he said quietly. "I am going to switch chairs and take Fritter for a walk.

"Want company," asked Dawn.

"Sure."

Allen went inside to grab a jacket and switch to his trail wheelchair. He gave a call out to the others in the house, which was unusual because he liked to go for walks with Fritter on his own most evenings. As he grabbed Fritter's leash from the hook by the door he was a little surprised to find not only Dawn, but Bjorn, Shelia, Kelly, and Amar waiting to join them.

"Baba said we needed to walk off the big supper," said Amar. "Where we going?"

Fritter had heard her leash being taken off its hook and she was sitting outside the screen door, her tail eagerly thumping against the boards of the deck.

"I think Fritter is leading the way," said Allen as he pushed open the door and hooked the leash to the Basset Hound.

Before he could sit up straight, Fritter was off, dragging Allen behind her. Allen's wheelchair almost toppled as Fritter took a sharp turn at the bottom of the ramp. The others quickly followed. Fritter didn't slow down. She headed straight for the west end of the street, ears and jowls flapping as she pulled Allen behind her. The Basset Hound looked like she could trip over her ears at any moment. She would have headed straight into the woods if Allen hadn't grabbed hold of the rims on his wheels to slow her down.

The MacIver kids found themselves at the entrance to the trails where they last encountered the aliens. A tall chain link fence had been erected there immediately after people had seen what was once a hill, lift into the sky and disappear. The entire area had been closed off for what the public was told were "safety reasons". According to the media coverage, people had not seen a spacecraft, but a "large volume of debris that has been thrown into the sky from an explosion of gases that had filled empty aqueducts." They were told that what looked like a space craft flying away was merely the lighter debris being caught by the wind.

"The gates are open," said Kelly as she walked closer to read a new sign that had been posted.

Kelly started reading but Fritter wasn't waiting. She headed off at full speed through the open gate, pulling her leash out of Allen's hand. Allen looked at the others, shrugged, then followed Fritter, the rest of the kids close behind. They quickly lost sight of Fritter, but with her hound dog call as she ran, Fritter was pretty easy to follow. When they caught up to her, Fritter was lying down at the end of a trail overlooking a valley where there was once a hill.

"This looks like it has been this way forever," said Sheila. "How could everything grow back so quickly? There are even fully grown trees!"

"You would think that with all those people and machines that had up here, it would look more like a gravel pit than a valley that had been untouched," added Kelly.

"You think we are supposed to be here?" asked Bjorn.

"They left the gates open," replied Allen.

Allen started to say something else when he noticed Fritter raise her head and look as alert as a Basset Hound could. He looked around and couldn't see anything, but he felt the hair on his arms rise.

"We aren't alone," said Allen quietly.

The five other MacIvers moved in closer to Allen, looking around. Fritter picked that time to lay her head on the ground before casually rolling onto her side.

"I did not mean to scare you."

All six of the MacIvers jumped at the sound of the voice in the trees beside them.  Fritter grunted as she rolled over onto her back, all four paws to the sky, lazily watching Pinqua emerge from the trees. The alien casually walked up to the MacIvers, pausing to look them over.

"Where are the rest of you?"

"We thought you were gone," said Allen as he pushed his way around Amar who stood between him and the alien.

"I was, but now I am back, and we need your help once more."

Pinqua looked at the children in front of him and realized they were not prepared.  Despite him trying to communicate with Allen for weeks, it was clear that the messages had never got through.

"Sit," he said as he motioned to the kids.

Pinqua told the MacIvers that he and his people had got safely away from the Earth and the Loma.  His people were doing much better and by now were likely home.  During their journey, they were contacted by friends who were in distress. The MacIvers were the only ones capable of providing the help his friends needed.

"What kind of friends?" asked Kelly.

Pinqua paused as if choosing his words carefully, before speaking.

"They are much like you.  They lived here among you in plain sight at one time," said Pinqua.

"And where do they live now?" asked Amar cautiously.

"Not here.  Not on your planet," said Pinqua as he looked toward the setting sun. "Jupiter."

"Yeah, I don't think so," said Kelly firmly.  "First you almost get one of us killed, then you want us to spend what? Like six years flying to some planet to help some creatures that used to live here!"

The MacIvers looked at their sister.  They were familiar with what that red head tone of voice meant.

"What?" said Kelly firmly.  "So I did some research and learned something.  There is no way we are just up and leaving for six years there and six years back, and who knows how long on some planet that is just a bunch of gas we can't even breathe.  I am going home. You guys should come too."

Kelly got up off the ground and without another word, walked away and towards home.  No one tried to stop her because they were all familiar with her temper.

"Not six years," said Pinqua.  "Your sister would be right if we were traveling using your technology, but we would not be.  She is also right about you not being able to live on Jupiter, but we are not going to the planet, we are going to its moon.

"Tells us more," said Allen.

Pinqua explained that their technology allowed them to travel at more than 10% the speed of light using an anti-matter drive. That meant that they could be at their destination in less than a day. Pinqua pleaded with Allen and the others to come with him to help, but it had to be all of the MacIver kids.

"I can not explain why it has to be all of you, but I think if you look at yourselves you will find that as a group you have some unique abilities together," said Pinqua. "This is your calling."

Pinqua was interrupted by the sound of some voices coming up the path. The kids turned to look in the direction of the voices and by the time they had turned back, Pinqua was gone. A young couple rounded the corner on the path and was a little startled to see the MacIvers sitting there.

"Oh, wow. We didn't expect to run into anyone up here. We just saw them open the gates today and thought we would have a look around," said the man who the kids recognized from down the road a few houses. "Doesn't look like much has changed for all the construction crews that were in here."

Sheila got up and retrieved Fritter's leash.

"Pretty much the same as it was before," said Sheila. "Let's go guys, before it gets too late."

The MacIver Kids headed down the path towards home, leaving the couple to enjoy their walk.

"How did they not notice an entire hill missing," whispered Amar as he walked alongside Allen. Allen just shrugged his shoulders.

# Chapter 2

Kelly was waiting on the porch when Allen, Amar, Dawn, Bjorn, and Shelia, arrived home. Brad, Antonia, Joane, and Deane were all waiting with her.

"Treehouse," said Allen firmly as he undid the clasp on Fritter's leash.

It didn't take long for the MacIver kids to gather in the tree house, but it took a while for them to all quiet down.

"I think this might be my fault," said Allen. "I have been hearing a voice and dreaming weird dreams for a while now. I just thought they were because of the weird stuff we have been through, but I think that was Pinqua trying to communicate."

"You can't seriously be suggesting we go away for years, Allen."

Kelly still had a tone of fire in her voice.

"Less than a day to get there," said Amar. "Something about an anti-matter engine or something like that."

"Really," exclaimed Kelly, exchanging her tone of fire for one of excitement and interest.

"We all need to go," said Allen. "Not just some of us. All of us."

There was a lot of discussion and debate that followed. Everyone listed reasons why they couldn't go and at times got into almost heated arguments over whether those were valid reasons or not. There was a moment of silence between the discussions and some of the kids noticed Allen holding his arm out straight in front of him. He wasn't saying or doing anything, just holding his arm straight out, hand open, palm to the floor. Bjorn stood up and put his hand over Allen's and Antonia did the same, putting her hand over Bjorn's.

One by one the other kids noticed and followed the lead. First Dawn, then Deane and Sheila, then Joane and Kelly, and finally Brad putting his hand on the top of the pile. The moment Brad's hand touched the other each of the MacIver kids felt a warmth and energy flow through them. They stood silently, basking in the feel of that energy.

"This is why it has to be all of us," said Allen. "I don't understand it yet, but together there is something special about us. So, do we go, or do we stay?"

"I thought we were all putting our hands in to vote to go," said Brad.

Antonia pulled her hand out of the stack of hands and used it to smack Brad playfully on the back of the head. As soon as she did a chill wafted over the kids and they all dropped their hands.

"You are so dense sometimes," said Antonia. "Don't you remember when Mom used to make us do that so we would all be quiet and pay attention."

"We all good then," asked Allen as he moved to the swing to lower himself out of the treehouse.

Everyone silently nodded.

"I will go talk with Baba then, and hope he can convince Nani," said Allen. "We leave tonight."

In the house Allen found Amar's grandparents sitting at the kitchen table drinking chai, which Nani seemed to have a perpetual pot of on the stove. He was surprised to see a third mug on the table as though they were expecting company.

"That is for you Allen," said Nani. "Something good for you to remember you have something to come home to."

Allen looked a little shocked as he reached for his mug of chai. He watched Baba carefully, but the old man kept a straight face. He could only hold a straight face for a moment though before breaking out in laughter at the shocked look on Allen's face.

"I tell her everything," said Baba. "No secrets. It was her son too that was taken."

"But how do you know?" asked Allen.

"When you get old your hearing goes, but in that silence, you learn to listen to different things. Your friend has spoken with me as well, but he insisted I let you figure it out on your own."

The three of them sat quietly, enjoying their chai. When Allen set his empty mug on the table and started to back away, Nani reached for him, putting her hand on his.

"Amar is our heart; you and the others are all my family. Come back safe please."

Allen wasn't quite sure how to respond so he just nodded his head.

"We will cover with your parents as long as we can, but you should be prepared with an explanation when you return."

Again Allen nodded. He wasn't prepared for that conversation with his parents.

The MacIver kids all gathered in the living room. There was a nervous tension that they could all feel. They wear eager to make their way to Pinqua, but the neighbourhood was still alive with activity and they didn't want to raise any attention. It was close to midnight when the kids got up and made their way to the door. Allen stopped to cuddle Fritter and whispered in the dog's ear.

"Take care of them."

As if she completely understood, Fritter walked over and laid down at Baba's feet.  One by one the kids stepped out the doorway into the night and they made their way to the paths at the end of their street.  When they got there they found the gate closed but whoever had locked it up was apparently not paying attention as the lock had not been closed properly.  Brad opened the gate and when everyone was through, he closed it back up, reaching through the chain link to replace the lock the same way they found it.  He scanned down the road to see if anyone might have seen them but there was no movement in the neighbourhood.

No one had thought to bring a flashlight, and they had all left their cell phones at home figuring they would not need them where they were going, but also so Baba could watch for any text messages from their parents and cover for them.  The pathways that used to be gravel and natural trails had been paved while the area was closed off so with the little moonlight there was the kids were able to follow the path relatively easily.

"You need to move faster.  They know you are here."

Allen felt the voice more than he heard it.

"Gotta move guys," said Allen as he bore down on the rims of his tires with a big push.  Almost in unison, the MacIver kids broke into a jog.  As they rounded the corner they saw a lit doorway at the edge of the trees.  Allen headed straight for the doorway and the rest of the kids followed.  Bjorn was the last one through the door.  He turned to look back and saw several deer on the path they had just stepped off of.

"Look," Bjorn said, but before the others could turn to see what he was pointing at the door closed.

A small group of soldiers rounded the corner the MacIvers had just come around. They deer immediately perked up as the light from the powerful flashlights washed over them. One of the soldiers stepped forward and the deer bounded off into the trees with barely a sound.

"Let me see that thing," said one of the soldiers as he grabbed a device from another. "Are you telling me we were just chasing down a bunch of damn deer?"

Inside the ship the MacIvers could not hear the commotion outside as soldiers spread out to search and radios blared as a soldier controlling a silent drone overhead tried to explain how he could have mistaken the deer for people. It didn't take long for the soldiers to wrap up their search and leave.

"This is amazing," said Joane as she ran her hand over the walls. "It feels like a turtle shell. Feel it! It almost feels alive."

"That is because it is," said Pinqua as he appeared.

Antonia ran over and gave Pinqua a hug, which seemed to surprise the alien momentarily.

"I am so glad you are well. How is everyone?"

"Thanks to you, they are doing well."

Pinqua stepped out of Toni's hug and he motioned for the kids to follow.

"We need to wait a bit before we leave, so I will show you around."

Pinqua guided them around the inside of the spacecraft which seemed surprisingly large. The alien answered the abundance of questions the kids had, most of them coming from Kelly as she probed Pinqua for the details on the technical aspects of the ship. Pinqua patiently explained how the ship used particle accelerators to produce anti-matter that was stored in a very specialized containment system that lets the anti-matter be stored safely for long periods. Magnetic traps were used to keep the anti-matter from making contact with the ship's structure. By controlling the release of the anti-matter the ship created thrust and could reach speeds faster than 10% the speed of light.

"Is that like warp drive," asked Brad.

Pinqua gave Brad a strange look.

"He watched too much TV," said Kelly. "He thinks he is in an episode of Star Trek."

The alien paused for a moment, looking off and up to the right.

"Ahhh…now I get the reference," said the alien. "Brad may be correct to a degree. This journey could very much be like one of your science fiction movies, but it is reality, so no warp drive, only anti-matter."

Pinqua returned to his explanation of how the ship worked.  As he did so some of the kids wandered off and found a place to sit down, but Kelly was digging for information and Pinqua seemed to be enjoying providing that information.  He explained how the anti-matter propulsion system was able to deliver an extremely high specific impulse, getting them to speed with extreme ease. On longer journeys, the ship would use the anti-matter drive to get up to speed and then deploy sails. He also described how the biggest risk to them was from high-energy radiation.

"Which is why this is part of the ship," said Pinqua as he reached out and stoked the wall which seemed to shimmer all around them in response.  "The wall is alive with a creature that feeds on that radiation and neutralizes it. It has a symbiotic relationship with the ship, feeding on the radiation, while providing a structure and shielding to the ship."

Kelly stroked the wall and the small area she touched shimmered.  She was disappointed that the entire wall didn't shimmer like it had when Pinqua had stroked it.

"This creature is also like your chameleons.  It adapts and blends into its surroundings seamlessly, which is why this ship can hide in plain sight.

The talk of the walls of the ship being alive had caught the attention of the rest of the MacIvers.  They all tried touching the walls to see if they could get it to shimmer, but like Kelly, only the small area beneath their hand reacted, except when Allen touched the wall.  As he did so every surface around them shimmered and almost glowed. Before anyone could say anything Pinqua touched the screen on a control panel and 10 chairs emerged from the floor.

"Take a seat. It is time we leave," Pinqua directed.

Each of the MacIver kids grabbed a seat and as they did so a harness locked them in. Allen was setting the locks on his wheels so he could transfer into the last chair and was surprised to see clamps raise out of the floor and grip the tires of the wheelchair. He lifted himself over into the chair that had come out of the floor and found it surprisingly comfortable despite how it looked. He panicked for a brief moment as the harness wrapped around him but quickly relaxed.

"I must apologize for this," said Pinqua as the kids felt their seats warm slightly and gentle vibrations coursing through their bodies. "You will all be asleep rather quickly. The effects of gravitational time dilation can be disturbing to some so this is the best alternative."

Kelly started to object but sleep caught up to her first.

The ship silently lifted into the sky. The drone that had remained flying over the area watching for any activity found itself caught up in the air currents and went spinning out of control. The drone operator was caught off guard at the sudden change and tried desperately to regain control, only to watch helplessly as it crashed into the side of a building.

Pinqua double-checked the MacIvers before engaging the full force of the anti-matter drive. Allen closed his eyes tightly and acted as though he too were asleep but knew his deception had been caught when he felt Pinqua's hand on his shoulder.

"This would be a good time for us to talk," said Pinqua before tapping his screen and sending the spaceship toward Jupiter.

# Chapter 3

The MacIvers woke up almost in unison. They were disoriented at first, but as they took their settings in, they remembered that they had boarded a spaceship the night before. The question was, where were they now? The harnesses that had held them down were gone and if the ship was moving they couldn't feel it. They all felt surprisingly refreshed and well. Pinqua was nowhere to be found.

"Where is Allen," asked Deane.

The others quickly scanned the room and were relieved when Allen wheeled through a doorway into the room.

"Good," said Allen. "You are finally awake. Come on. They are waiting for us."

The MacIver kids followed Allen out of the spaceship and into a brightly lit area. It took a few moments for their eyes to adjust, and when they did the kids still barely noticed the group of people waiting for them.

"Holy…"

"Don't you dare say that word, Bradley MacIver," said Dawn firmly.

Brad caught himself as he stood slack-jawed looking up at what was definitely not the sky.

"Are we the goldfish in the bowl," asked Joane.

A large dome surrounded them and outside the dome swam creatures that looked like animals out of the Paleozoic Era display they had seen at the Royal Tyrrell Museum. Bjorn reached for a small notebook he always carried in his pocket to make quick sketches and remembered that he had changed before he left the house, forgetting his notebook in his other pants.

"This might help," said a young girl has she reached out with what looked like a sketchpad and pencil.

Antonia noticed this, and then quickly realized there was a large group of people around them.  She tapped Brad on the shoulder to get his attention and the other MacIver within her reach.

"I am sorry," said Antonia.  "We haven't seen anything quite like this and didn't notice you."

A young man stepped out from the group and shook Antonia's hand using a wrist clasp.

"I am Leonidas," said the Man.

"I am…"

Leonidas interrupted her.

"You are Antonia. And this is Dawn," said Leonidas, as he reached to shake her hand. "Bjorn, Deane, Sheila, Amar, Joane, Kelly," continued Leonidas as he shook each of their hands.

"Allen," he said, shaking his hand a little longer. "And of course you are Brad," said Leonidas, sounding almost excited while shaking Brad's hand firmly and vigorously.

Brad had a strange feeling as he looked at Leonidis, but he could quite figure out what that feeling was. The other MacIver kids watched curiously as Brad appeared to be shaking hands with a mirror image of himself.

"Where exactly are we," asked Brad, trying to interrupt his feeling of confusion.

"Ah, yes. Follow me," said Leonidas "There is much to see and talk about."

As Leonidas led the way the others who had gathered approached the kids, greeting them and handing them food, which the MacIvers eagerly took. They walked through a tunnel that seemed to be lit by bioluminescence and emerged at the edge of a thriving city like none the MacIvers had ever seen. The entire city was under a dome.

"This is Atlantis," said Leonidas, making a large sweeping gesture with his arm.

"Wait a minute," said Deane. "Do you mean like the mythological lost continent on Earth?"

Leonidas smiled as he looked back at the MacIvers.

"No, my friend. Atlantis is neither mythological nor lost. It is right here, on Europa."

The light was unfamiliar to the MacIver kids. It took some time for their eyes to adjust, though Brad seemed to adapt quicker than the others. The architecture of the city, which appeared to be a bustling metropolis, was a symphony of glowing structures and bioluminescent flora. As they walked along the catwalk the MacIvers watched Atlanteans moving through the streets below, their clothing iridescent and shimmering like the scales of marine creatures. Were it not for the strange bioluminescent light, and the gigantic dome over their heads, this would look just like any busy city on Earth.

The dome, which had no supporting structure, appeared as though it were not there at all. The water above them looked like it was just holding itself back above the city by its own choice. The water ranged in color from a rich azure to dark indigo. Most of the MacIvers assumed at first that it was just the sky above them until they saw marine life swimming around and gentle ripples rolling up and along the dome over the top of them.

Many of the buildings seemed almost transparent, mimicking the shimmering effect they could see on the creatures swimming outside the dome. Much of the city looked as though it was a giant coral with buildings that had organic, flowing shapes, with textured surfaces like coral. The colors were amazing and bright, with vibrant hues.

"The entire city looks like one of those ornaments you see in a salt-water aquarium," said Bjorn.

Among the coral-like structures were crystal atriums. From their vantage point, the MacIvers could see that some of these atriums housed gardens and recreation areas. The tallest buildings were all characterized by their spiral designs that looked like gigantic conch cells. There was one building in the center of the city that drew the attention of all the MacIvers. It rose from the floor of the city and looked as though it pierced the dome.

"What is that place," asked Brad.

"That is the Aqua Nexus. It is where we harness the power of the ocean currents above us and the geothermal vents below," replied one of the Atlanteans walking with them.

"Wow," Kelly said, speaking much louder than she had intended.

"We would be pleased to show it to you," replied the Atlantean who had identified the building.

"Priorities," said Leonidas quite firmly.

"Yes, of course…"

The Atlantean stepped back from the MacIvers in response to the chastisement.

Leonidas guided the MacIvers to one of the spiral towers.  As they walked through the tower, they saw rooms full of lab workers, one that housed what looked like electronic panels, and yet another that looked very much like a library.

"Is this a university?  Or a school of some sort?" asked Antonia, thinking back to a recent tour of a university she took with her mother.

Leonidas leaned over and spoke to the individuals beside him briefly.

"Ah yes," he exclaimed as he turned to face Antonia. "Each of the spiral buildings you saw is a place of study and learning.  Now come sit down."

The doorway in front of them didn't really open.  There was no sideways or up-and-down movement.  The MacIvers weren't quite sure where the doors went, but through the doorway there was a large boardroom-style table with many chairs around it.  Everyone was soon seated, and more food was brought for the MacIvers to eat.

"I know you have many questions," said Leonidas.  "It is understandable.  You have come to help us, but one thing we hold dear in our culture is that our history is as valuable as our present.  I ask for your patience and indulgence for a short time, please."

On the table in front of them, a three-dimensional image of the Earth appeared.  Leonidas moved his hands and zoomed into the image.

"I know this may not look like it, but this is your Earth, almost 12,000 years ago."

Leonidas paused to the kids take in what they were seeing. Deane was fascinated and reached out, discovering that as she moved her hand she shifted the image in front of her. She quickly pulled her hand away. Leonidas zoomed in closer on the image.

"That's Greece," whispered Sheila to her sister.

Leonidas smiled and began his tale of the history of the Atlanteans.

Atlanteans were not from Earth, but from somewhere far outside Earth's solar system. Their travels took them to Earth just as the ice-age ended and they set down just outside of modern-day Greece. Atlantis was a great empire, but our technology and influence were having a profound impact on the nations around it. One day, while the skies were filled with the smoke and soot of a nearby volcano, Atlantis closed its dome and lifted off seeking a new home and eventually settling on Europa.

"Wait a minute," said Deane. "Why do all the stories say Atlantis fell into the sea?"

"Because humankind has a need to have a logical explanation for things that defy their personal logic," said Leonidis.

"The entire island?" questioned Amar.

"It was never an island," said Leonidis. It was our ship when we landed there and our ship when we left there. As you have seen, Atlanteans are skilled at adapting to their environment. What you see here was, at one time, the central city which was surrounded by rings of land and water. Those rings were created from the force of our landing."

"Why here?" asked Allen, breaking what was a long silence in the room.

"It was our intention to go further, but one of the leaders became ill while they explored the planet you call Jupiter. The were dependant on him to fly the ship, but the stories passed down tell us he died talking about a dragon. Our ship attempted to set down on the surface of Europa, but the heat of our engines melted the ice, and this is where we came to rest," explained Leonidis.

"One person dies and your ship cannot fly?" questioned Kelly.

"Which is why we need your help."

A young woman came forward carrying a large book. She flipped through the pages as she explained the genealogy of the people that appeared on the pages and how they fit within the Atlantean culture. Up until the death of that one leader, their culture had always been led by the heads of one of three families. It took a decision of the Three in complete agreement for any significant changes to take place. This was built right into the controls for the ship which required genetic confirmation to activate and maneuver.

"Didn't he have children?" asked Sheila.

"His family had developed an attachment to your planet. When we left, they all stayed behind, so there was no lineage on board the ship." Explained the woman.

All eyes in the room turned to Brad, who felt extremely uncomfortable with the attention.

"You are the last of that line, Brad," said Leonidis. "And this is why we need you," he said as he placed one of the lost struts off the Galileo Space Probe onto the table in front of them.

# Chapter 4

The MacIvers were still unclear about how that carbon fiber strut had made it from space to Europa and through the ice. Their level of commitment to the environment they lived in though led to the debris being found on the ocean floor, and that led to many questions from the Atlanteans. They had not been in contact with Earth since they had left it, but this discovery led to them utilizing their technology to find out what was happening above the ice. It didn't take long for the Atlanteans to determine that Europa was about to be visited by people from Earth which would lead to their discovery.  It was time for them to move again.

As they exited the spiral tower to one of the many cat walks, the city had noticeably changed from when they had arrived.  It was dark like the sun had gone down, but of course, there was no sun.  When they looked up, bioluminescent creatures that had attached themselves to the dome looked like stars in a night sky.  The Atlanteans accompanying them waited patiently while the MacIver kids took in the sight.

The kids were led to a group of rooms in a nearby building.  To the MacIver kids, it felt like they were being put up in an apartment of their own.  All the sleeping spaces opened onto a large common room that was covered by a crystal dome that made the light in the room dance.

"I hope this is okay," said a young Atlantean girl shyly. "We tried to make sure everything you need is in here."

"I am sure it will be fine," said Antonia.  "It is beautiful."

"Our city rises early.  You are welcome to leave this place and go where you wish.  There are a few places that are sealed for safety, but there is nowhere you can't go."

"Is there a phone or something we can use to call someone if we need something?" asked Joane.

"We have technology that will do that, but we highly value face-to-face communication and avoid intrusions into our peace.  If you need anything, please knock on one of the adjacent doors in the building.  All will help you if they can," said the young girl. "If you go out and find yourself lost, just ask anyone for help.  It is a big city, but I am confident that everyone already knows who you are."

The girl closed the door behind her as she left.  Amar waited a moment or two before going to the door and testing it.  To his surprise, he found that they had not been locked in.  The kids were quiet as they settled into the space.  Sheila and Deane looked through the kitchen and found some food which they set out.  Allen toured the apartment, checking in with each of his brothers and sisters as he did so. He was about to sit with the group of them that had gathered around the food when he realized he had not seen Brad for a while. He quickly rolled through the apartment looking for Brad when he noticed a door open that hadn't been earlier. Allen rolled up to the door and found Brad standing on a deck looking over the city. He rolled up beside Brad, set his brakes, and leaned up against the rail to see the city below, never saying a word. The two of them stood like that for a long time.

It wasn't long before the stress of the day caught up with the MacIver kids. They each made their way to the room they had picked up and were soon asleep. They woke to the sounds of the city coming to life.

"You sleep okay, Brad?" asked Antonia.

"No."

Antonia waited for Brad to add to his one-word answer, but when it seemed like he had nothing to add she got up to check on the others.

"Am I supposed to go away with them?" Brad blurted. "Because I can't do that."

Antonia sat back down, and the other kids overhearing Brad, came and sat with him. Each of the kids was as adamant as Brad about him not going with them. There was even talk about leaving and returning home immediately, which many of the kids agreed with until Dawn asked a question.

"How would we get home?  We haven't even seen Pinqua since we fell asleep on his spaceship."

The was a brief silence, and many of their kids looked to Allen for an answer.

"We can leave when we want," said Allen.  "We are not prisoners on this planet.  But I think we need to take some time to find out what is really expected."

A strange sound filled the room.  It was Sheila who thought it sounded similar to a doorbell, so she went to the door and opened it as they had been shown.  A group of Atlanteans were on the other side of the door carrying trays.

"Good morning.  We live across the hall and thought that you might be interested in some breakfast.  Being your first morning here, we guessed that you might not be familiar.  Atlanteans don't normally keep a lot of food in storage, so we picked you up some this morning," said the woman as she invited herself in and set her tray on a table. The others followed her.

"This is a remarkable drawing," said the man, as he moved the sketch Bjorn had been working on off to the side.

Antonia got up and helped the woman remove some dishes from a cabinet.

"Thank you for the food," said Antonia.  "I am not sure how we pay you for it though."

The Atlantean woman looked confused and glanced at her husband who looked just as confused.  It was the young boy with them that came to the rescue.

"We just learned this, Mom," the boy said excitedly. "On Earth, we used to exchange metal coins for goods.  I think that is what she means."

The woman laughed and took hold of Antonia's hands.

"We do not…, pay I think was the word you used, for food.  There is plenty for everyone. Now everyone come eat."

The MacIver kids gathered eagerly around the food. Much of it looked strange to them, but the Atlanteans who discovered was a family just being neighbourly, tried their best to explain what the food was.  The explanations didn't help much, but the kids were hungry enough that they tried a bit of everything.

"We have to attend to our service requirements for the day, so we must be going," said the man. "Bjorn, my work is teaching the creation and preservation of art works.  Would you be interested in perhaps joining me today? Perhaps show us how you do works like this, "he asked as he held up Bjorn's sketch.

Bjorn looked to Antonia, and then Allen, for some direction. Both of them nodded so he eagerly accepted the invitation.

"Excellent.  Alexendar," the man said, pointing to the young boy that had come in with them, "must attend his place of learning, but if you like, Iris would be pleased to be your guide through our city.”

“Thank you. We would really appreciate that,” said Brad, as he moved forward to shake the girl's hand. Antonia gave Brad a bit of a side-eye look, but nobody in the room seemed to catch it.

Iris appeared to be close to Brad’s and Antonia’s age, though it was difficult to tell. She had exceptionally long dark hair, as almost all of the women they had seen on Atlantis had. Her deep brown eyes matched the color of her skin. Unlike the girls in the MacIver family, her face and body were full and curvaceous, and she carried herself proudly. It was clear to Antonia that Brad was enchanted by her.

Iris showed the MacIvers how to clean up the dishes they used and how to properly dispose of food waste. With confidence that belied her age, Iris went around to each room and explained to each of the MacIvers how to properly prepare their room before leaving for the day, letting the kids do the work on their own. At Bjorn's room, Iris quickly went through the room since Bjorn had left with her father.

“First thing,” said Iris as the MacIvers gathered to go tour the city. “We need to get you some clothes.”

“I have a question,” said Dawn. If Atlanteans are from ancient Greece, why do you all speak English?”

“English?” Iris said questionably.

“The language we speak,” said Brad.

"There was a mandate, many years ago when the artifact was found, that we all learn this language. It wasn't really hard as there are many similarities to ours."

As they exited the building they were in, they entered a street that was busy with people and vehicles. Amar found himself being pulled back off the roadway by a random person walking past, just in time to avoid a vehicle driving by.

"Thank you," Amar said, a little taken aback.

"Did you not hear it coming," asked the person who had grabbed him.

Amar shook his head and looked at the other kids, all of whom agreed that they didn't hear the vehicle.

"Do all these vehicles make sounds you here?" asked Joane.

"They are quite noisy," said the person as he looked across to Iris. "Curious."

With that, they walked off, as though they had somewhere to be.

"That is curious," said Iris. "Your hearing seems different from ours."

"Or maybe it's too much loud rock music," said Brad.

Iris turned to face Brad.

"You make music with rocks?"

Brad laughed. All the MacIvers did, but Brad a little more than the others.

"No. It's a style of music," said Antonia.

Iris shrugged her shoulders and led the kids through the street. Antonia gave Brad a little shove to get his attention.

"You are being a little obvious, Brad."

Brad gave his sister a bit of a dirty look and ignored her. Their first stop brought them up against the dome. The MacIvers all pushed up against the clear structure and looked out. To their surprised the city was not sitting directly on the ocean floor, but above it. There were other smaller domes outside of the dome, all raised on coral-like stilts that blended in seamlessly with the surrounding environment. Between the structures, people were moving around working alongside some equipment.

"Are those people out there?" asked Amar.

Iris nodded.

"In every movie I have seen Atlanteans have gills and can breathe in the water."

"What is a movie?" asked Iris.

"Do you guys record images over time of your experiments in the labs, or your activities?" asked Allen.

Iris nodded again.

"Movies are like that, only they are creative stories, not reality."

"I see," said Iris as she placed herself between Brad and Antonia and pointed out the workers below, explaining what they were doing.

The reality of Atlanteans was much less dramatic than the movies portrayed, at least when it came to working and moving through water. Their high-tech diving suits were made from advanced materials that were sleek, lightweight, and able to protect the users from the high pressure and the cold. The helmets were made from the same material as the dome, giving the impression that they were not wearing any helmets at all. Inside the helmets, the users wore a set of glasses that adapted to whatever light was available allowing them to see everything easily. The glasses also showed messages and communications to the wearer.

The suits did not have oxygen tanks. They had a rebreathing system that utilized a combination of technology and living organisms to filter exhaled air and convert it into useable oxygen. Some of the suits were equipped with integrated propulsion systems and tools, and each suit was customized to the wearer and that wearer's specific tasks.

The workers they were watching were farming. The seaweed they were farming was a primary component of much of the food Atlanteans ate. As the workers completed their tasks, a variety of fish and other marine life swam among them.

"I heard you were over here."

It was Helen, the woman who had told them about the Aqua Nexus the day before.

"Iris, it is nice to see you being such a genial host to our guests," said Helen.

Iris bowed her head in acknowledgment and held her head bowed for a long time.

"Kelly, I am on my way to the Aqua Nexus, which I know holds some interest for you.  Would you like to join me?" asked Helen.

"Yes please," replied Kelley excitedly.

"Walk with me then," said Helen who quickly turned and started walking away.  Kelly quickly caught up and joined her.

It wasn't until Helen had moved away that Iris raised her head.  Brad looked at her curiously.

"Are you okay," Brad asked.

"Helen is the leader of one of the Three families.  While we pretend to be an advanced society of respect and equality, the caste system is still engrained and we are expected to act in an appropriate way," replied Iris.

"Hmmm," replied Brad.

"Some things never change," said Amar.  "My grandparents told me similar stories of their home."

"You and your family do not have to worry about this

Brad.  You are one of the Three."

Brad stood up tall and faced Iris directly.

"I am nobody special.  If it weren't for the rest of my family, who accept me as one of them even though we all come from different families, I would likely be less than a nobody."

Brad paused, looking at his brother and sisters, then turned to look outside the dome.  Antonia knew the look outside the dome was to hide the tear in the corner of his eye.

"I don't know if you were told to treat me special, or my family, but please don't.  If there is one thing the MacIvers know, it is that not one of us is any better than anyone else."

Iris waited for Brad to turn back, and nodded silently.

They next stop on the tour was what appeared to be a marketplace but the absence of workers selling the many items available told a different story. The MacIver kids found it odd that in a place that looked similar to their local shopping mall, people would simply walk in, grab an item or two, and walk out.  It didn't make a difference if it was food or clothing, containers or tools.

Iris explained that one of the key values of Atlantean culture was that no person goes without.  Everyone had a role in their society, and they were expected to fulfill that role, but they did not receive any specific compensation for it.  All the necessities for living and surviving were made available for free.  There were repercussions for those who took more than needed, but Iris had not heard of any in her time.

"Seems too good to be true," said Sheila skeptically.

"It works during good times," said Iris.  "There have been periods in our history when there were difficulties and shortages, and it has not worked so well for some groups."

Iris engaged the help of a few other Atlanteans to help find clothes for the MacIver kids.  It felt like a shopping trip with their parents before going back to school for another year as they were encouraged to go try on the clothes picked for them and model the clothes.

Antonia bent over as she turned Allen's wheelchair around and whispered in his ear. "Watch."

Brad came out of a changing area in the clothes that Iris had picked out for them.  Iris made him walk and spin like a model.  As she adjusted his top Iris winked at Brad which brought a huge smile to Brad's face, until Brad noticed Allen and Antonia watching and his smile quickly turned into an embarrassed red face.

When they left the market they were wearing their new clothing, and their old clothing was being brought back by someone else to their apartment.

As the MacIvers approached their building after a full morning of touring Antonia noticed a symbol on a building that looked like the Caduceus, a symbol commonly associated with medical professions on Earth. This one was slightly different though with a single serpent coiled around a staff, without wings.

"What is that symbol?" Antonia asked.

"That is the Rod of Asclepius," a man answered from behind her. "That building is what we call an Asclepion, a place where we treat the sick."

"A hospital," said Antonia.

The man was standing beside Antonia now.

"I have heard that you have some skill with treating the sick, Antonia. Would you like to see it?"

"You guys go home," directed Antonia. "I can find my way back when I am done here."

# Chapter 5

There was no sound or knock. Leonardis simply walked into the apartment the MacIvers were staying in unannounced. He sat himself down beside Sheila and Deane who were in the common area on their own. He said nothing, while he stared at the two girls, who felt very unsettled as he watched them. Brad walked into the room and intuitively understood his sisters' discomfort.

"I did not hear a bell or knock," said Brad.

"I let myself in," replied Leonidis. "As the leader of one of the Three, it is common practice."

Brad placed himself between Leonidis and his sisters.

"It may be, but for us, it is not," said Brad firmly. "In our culture it is intrusive, and an older man staring at younger women is not socially acceptable."

Amar entered the room as Brad was speaking. Leonidis stood up.

"I would take this as an offense if you were Atlantean."

Amar started to step forward, but Brad held his hand up, stopping him.

"We are here because you need our help. Mine specifically apparently. If that has changed we will leave. If it has not, then I trust you will respect our cultural differences as we will try to respect yours."

Leonidis took a step closer to Brad, but Brad didn't move.

"In the meantime, while we are here, our sisters will not be left on their own," said Brad, glancing over at Amar as he said it, who nodded in acknowledgment.

Leonidis stared Brad down for a short time, but Brad never wavered in his cold stare back.

"I came to invite you to my home so we could discuss a solution to the missing Third," said Leonidis as he turned abruptly and walked towards the door. "I will send someone around to pick you up in a while."

Allen rolled into the room just as Leonidis walked out the door.

"What did I miss?"

"Bring everyone in here now," said Brad. There was a quiver in his voice, betraying the fear that he had hidden when he stood up to Leonidis. "Are you two okay?"

Sheila and Deane hugged Brad. They didn't say anything. They didn't need to. Allen gathered the MacIvers that were in the apartment and Iris who had been helping Joane do her hair in Atlantean-style braids. Kelly and Antonia had not yet returned to the apartment.

"I know you will think I am being my usual bossy self, but we," Brad said as he pointed at Allen and Amar, "need to make sure our sisters are never left alone. Especially with Leonidas."

"I don't understand," said Allen.

Brad searched for the wording to explain his fears without embarrassing his sisters or scaring them, but Iris spoke first.

"May I suggest that you may never understand. All you need to know is Brad is right," she said as she gently placed her hand on Brad's forearm.

"I get it," said Amar.

Allen looked confused for a few moments, then his eyes opened wide as he looked quickly from Brad to Deane and Sheila, and back.

"We're fine," said Sheila. "Brad made sure we were safe."

"I am sorry," said Allen. "I am sorry. I shouldn't have brought us here. I am sorry. We should find Toni and Kelly and go."

While he spoke, Allen moved in circles in his wheelchair, as if he were trying to figure out which way to go. He stopped moving when he felt Brad's firm grip on his shoulder.

"It's not your fault, bro," Brad said reassuringly. "Some people, apparently even those from advanced alien cultures are just a…" Brad caught himself before saying the word on his mind. "Jerks."

Allen didn't reply. He stared back at his brother.

"I know you are the brains of this operation," said Brad. "But how about you let me take the lead while we are here? We need you to help the rest of us figure out what to do."

"Done," said Allen. "We will follow your lead."

———————————

In the center of the city, Helen was taking Kelly on an extensive tour of the Aqua Nexus. They started by taking an elevator down to the ocean floor where large structures penetrated the ocean floor. Even at this level, the outer wall was clear, and Kelly could make out four legs that held the city high above the ocean floor. They were covered with coral and plant life, but unlike the space she was in, they were dark and metallic.

"Why are those structures different from everything else?" asked Kelly.

"Those are a part of the engines that enable the city to fly. The material that makes up our dome is incredibly strong, but it would not be able to withstand the temperatures created during take-off and flight."

"Can I see those?"

Helen gave a gentle laugh. "You are a curious one."

Helen explained the structures in front of them that penetrated the ocean floor. This was how they heated the city, using the structures to gather eat from a massive geothermal vent below the city. They directed that heat into water that flowed through tubes in the floor of the city and then up the sides of the dome, keeping the city at a constant temperature.

"The dome appears to be solid, but when you leaned against it you may have noticed it was warm. It is laced with tubes the heated water moves through. You just can't see the water moving against the background of the water outside."

Kelly tried to see the water moving in the walls of the dome, but she could not.

"You don't have to run pumps because the heated water naturally rises to the top."

"Impressive Kelly. You would make a fine engineer I think," said Helen.

"Is that what you are?"

"It is the path I was trained for when I was young. The patriarchs in my family passed without having male heirs so I am now one of the Three."

"So, men run this city?"

"Well, no, I am one of the Three," replied Helen in a cautious tone.

"But there are only two right now, and when you spoke out yesterday inviting me to see this you were shut down by Leonidis," said Kelly.

"You are an observant young woman. Atlantis is a patriarchal society. Had my father and grandfather not passed unexpectedly, I would not be one of the Three."

"Unexpectedly?" asked Kelly.

Helen seemed somewhat flustered by that question.

"Come along. There is much to see, Kelly."

Each level of the Aqua Nexus above the floor of the city had an elaborate garden in the center of it. The gardens were all part of an intricate that filtered the water from outside the dome into water that could be consumed by the Atlanteans. These same gardens also utilized the waste and sewage from the city to feed the plant life and cleaned what remained so it could be deposited outside of the city without causing harm to marine life or the environment.

At the very top of the Aqua Nexus a large spire project past the dome. The view from the top level of the Nexus let

Kelly observe the heated water leaving vents in the dome and travel up the sides of the spire. Kelly was able to see the interaction of the still warm water with the cold water of the ocean as she watched plants and small creatures caught up in the current the interaction created. The light from the spire, which did not have the same bioluminescent color as the other lights in the city, created a mesmerizing play of light and color through the currents and eddies around it. At the top of the spire was a device that looked just like a vertical windmill she had seen in books and on television at home.

"This is your generator!"

"Yes. I am surprised that you figured that out," said Helen. I would never have been able to do that at your age."

"But you said this is what you trained for."

"It was," said Helen. "But that does not mean I was good at it or liked it enough to take any real interest. Our paths are chosen for us."

Helen let those words sink in for Kelly for a moment or two.

"We have one last stop before returning you to your family."

The last stop was on the same level. It was a small, triangular-shaped room at the center of the top floor. Its walls were lined with dark screens, the ceiling a clear dome, and three chairs that looked like modern-day gaming chairs at the center of the room.

"This is the control center for our transportation mode. It has not been used since we settled here," said Helen.

"At all?" asked Kelly.

"I have no doubt that many of the Three have sat here and activated their controls over the many years," said Helen as she sat in one of the chairs.

The arms of the chair wrapped themselves around Helen's forearms and hands and the wall of dark screen opposite her came to life.

"At least in this chair and the one that belongs to Leonidis. Without the Third, it is of little use though. Which is why we need your brother. He is the last carrier of the genetics that will activate that chair."

---

Antonia stood back and watched the physicians at work. She did not understand many of the conversations going on around her but the doctor who was showing her around took time to answer her questions between his patient visits and interactions with his colleagues. Her first question was completely unrelated to the hospital.

"What language are you speaking?"

The doctor was a little surprised by the question but did his best to answer it.

"The language I can only describe as Atlantean. If you speak to almost anyone, they will be able to respond in your language because we were all compelled to learn it. Please understand that we are not trying to be poor hosts. It is only that your mask conceals who you are so the natural assumption is that you are one of us."

"I completely understand. I am not offended. I was just curious. Can I ask why everyone must wear a mask?" asked Antonia.

"They are to protect us, and protect others around us," explained the doctor.

He went on to explain how, despite the many medical and technological advances Atlanteans had made, living in a dome meant that microbes and airborne infections often circulated. Respiratory illnesses were the most common problems they saw, but some strains were far more deadly than others. It was not an uncommon occurrence for everyone in the city to be mandated to wear masks, and throughout their history, the entire city had been locked down several times.

"Atlantean culture is built on respect for each other, but it took some major changes in our education system for everyone to understand how, even though they showed no symptoms of illness, they could still be killing their friends and neighbors by not wearing a mask," added the doctor.

Antonia spent much of her time standing back and observing. The diagnostic equipment she saw used was similar in many ways to what she would have seen in a hospital on Earth, though there were some obvious technical advancements.  The treatments on the other hand seemed to abandon technology. A wide variety of plants were used to treat almost everything.  If there wasn't a plant treatment, they used something acquired from the marine life around them.  A man with a large cut on his thigh came in and the doctor invited Antonia over to help.

"What would you do?" asked the doctor.

"Tell him not to do it again," said Antonia, attempting to lighten the stress the man was exhibiting with a joke.

She thought the joke fell flat or was not understood until both men broke out in laughter.

"It looks deep," said Antonia, "but cleaning it out, stitching it, and maybe some antibiotics so it doesn't get infected."

"Stitching?  Like you do with clothes?" said the doctor curiously.

"Yeah, just like that," replied Antonia.

Both men broke out in laughter again.

"We have let it bleed freely to clear any debris out of the wound.  I can see how sewing it works, but we use these."

The doctor opened a small container that was crawling with tiny beetles. He reached into the container, picked up one of the beetles with some tweezers, and carefully placed it over one end of the wound. Antonia watched with fascination as the beetle bit down with its pincers, pulling the wound together. The injured man flinched a little and turned his head away.

"I hate bugs," he said.

"Then like Antonia said, don't do it again," said the doctor.

The doctor set several more beetles along the cut, one by one, until the wound was completely closed. As he did, he explained how when the beetle bit it injected a tiny bit of saliva that both numbed the area and kept other bad stuff away, which he assumed was the same as the antibiotics Antonia had mentioned. The beetles also consumed dead and damaged flesh which meant there was almost no scar tissue left behind when they dropped off on their own.

As Antonia accompanied the doctor the rest of the day, it was apparent that word got out who she was as people passing them greeted her in English. There was something odd that stood out to Antonia though.

"I don't think we have met any female doctors or nurses yet," commented Antonia.

"Women don't practice medicine," said the doctor matter of factly.

Antonia didn't probe any deeper.

———————————

Antonia and Kelly arrived back at the apartment just as Brad was returning from Leonidis' home. Brad didn't look happy, or well. Antonia and Kelly were surprised when he made his way to the door on the left when their apartment was on the right. Kelly tried to get Brad's attention, but he had already knocked on the door. Iris opened the door and greeted him.

"I need to know, and please answer me honestly," said Brad, not giving Iris a chance to say hello. "Are they listening to us inside that apartment? Are they spying on us?"

Iris looked to her mother who was now standing beside her. Her mother spoke quietly.

"They will always know where you are. Privacy is not something native to us. But with your doors and windows closed you can talk among each other without fear."

Brad listened carefully to the mother, but he watched Iris carefully.

"I am trusting you. Thank you."

Iris stepped back as the door closed. Brad and his sisters went to their apartment where they found the other MacIvers waiting for them.

"You won't believe…"

# Chapter 6

"You won't believe what they want me to do," said Brad as he practically stomped in the door.

He caught himself and looked back to make sure the door had closed behind him. He checked to see that the door to the deck was closed as well.

"A baby. A frickin' baby."

Antonia squinted and scrunched up her face as she processed what Brad had said.

"They want you to take care of a baby?" asked Dawn. "Like bring it back to Earth and be a dad?"

"No," said Brad, checking his tone as he knew he was getting loud. "As to make a baby and leave it here to the third."

"Holy…."

"Stop right there, Amar," said Kelly. "We are all thinking it, but we don't use those words."

"It makes sense," said Antonia. "You pass on your genetic code and then they don't need you to stay here."

"Well, you already found a girlfriend," said Allen, trying to lighten the moment a little.

"No," said Brad, completely ignoring the joke at his expense. "Leonidis says they have done genetic research and the best option if for me to have that baby with his daughter. I don't even have to touch her. They do some implant thing."

"Who else was there?" asked Kelly.

"What's that matter?"

"Just…who else was there when he told you this."

"It was just him and his son and daughter."

"I think we have a big problem here," said Kelly.

Kelly told the others about her day and what she had seen. She also told them about things she had learned by talking to Helen. After telling them about everything she saw and heard, Kelly explained that, to her, it seemed suspicious that the 'best way' to bring Brad's genetics back into the Atlantean society was through Leonidis' family because this would end with two families being in control instead of three.

"I also think that Helen thinks her father and grandfather were eliminated so that would leave Helen as the family leader and as a woman, with less influence than Leonidis."

"Women do seem to hold a lower place to men here," Antonia said. "They can't even work in medicine."

"Well, I wouldn't trust that man at all," said Deane. "Does his daughter even want to have your baby?

Brad had to stop and think. It was then that he realized that Leonidis' daughter had never said a word they entire time he was there.

"I am guessing not," said Brad.

"We can't let that happen," said Joane quietly. "There is something wrong here. It all looks too good on the surface, but I don't like it at all."

"There is something else," said Dawn. "Brad won't say it, but I know he thinks like us. None of us would abandon our children because we know not everyone is lucky enough to find a home like the MacIver's."

"I don't understand why we all had to come," added Sheila. "They only need Brad.

Allen sat back and listened to the others bounce their thoughts back and forth.  Brad was doing the same thing on the other side of the room. The conversation went on and on until Brad looked over at Allen with an exasperated look on his face.  Allen wheeled into the center of the kids which distracted them momentarily.

"So we have to get a submerged spaceship to fly so a hidden society can remain hidden. We have to do this without letting one man take control of everything.  And we have to do this while protecting the girls in our family, and possibly the entire city.  Does that about sum it up?" asked Allen.

"Yes," said Brad firmly. "And I am not being a part of making a baby."

"Agreed," said Antonia.

"We all had to come because we are stronger together and nobody takes better care of a MacIver than a MacIver," said Allen.  "So, let's step back, and hear about Bjorn's and Toni's day. Maybe they have pieces of the puzzle that will help us."

Bjorn didn't need much encouragement to talk about his day.  Iris' father was a professor at one of the many campuses throughout the city.  His specialty was the arts, and apparently, he was quite an accomplished artist of his own.  Bjorn got to sit in and paint with one of the classes.  As interesting as the arts were, the thing that was most interesting to him was the visit to a computer technology class, to listen to one of Iris' father's colleagues.

"He spoke about the code the city was based on," said Bjorn. "I am not really into that stuff. It doesn't make any sense to me. But the city runs on two separate systems. The one that allows the city to travel, and the new system that has been built up since they landed here, that controls everything else. The thing is, nobody knows how to change the old code, which is why they have never left here."

This got Allen's attention. Computer code was something he understood. In some ways the code and the math made more sense to him than language in general.

Antonia talked about her time in the medical center, and she took some pleasure in grossing out her siblings as she described how the beetles were used. She had found her time with the doctor quite pleasurable, and she was excited as she talked about learning about natural healing when she got home. She also told the MacIvers how the doctor felt completely comfortable telling her women didn't belong in medicine.

"And one more thing," said Antonia. "Respiratory illnesses are common here because it is all one big closed system. They wear masks in the medical center, but perhaps we should so we don't pick up a strange sickness, or worse, leave one behind."

It was getting late and the MacIvers were all tired. The lights had long since dimmed outside.

"Here is the plan for tomorrow," said Brad. "Number one. At no time do any of the girls go anywhere without Allen, Amar, or myself along. If it can't be avoided two or three of you stick together."

Brad looked at his sisters to see if he would get an argument, but there was none.

"Okay then, next. I don't know how we do this, but we need to get Allen near a computer so he can see that old code."

"You caught that, eh," said Allen.

"I did," said Brad. "Not just brawn. There are some brains there too."

"He just does a good job of keeping them hidden," said Joane.

The kids laughed, which was a nice light moment that they needed.

"Third, we need to see if we can find a way to hold a larger meeting, with more than just Leonidis and Helen. Maybe we can find out if people really support, or even know about Leonidis's plan," said Brad. "Now let's call it a night."

The MacIver kids made their way to their rooms, but Brad followed Allen to his room. There was more to the plan, but he wasn't ready to share it with everyone. Brad and Allen spent another hour or two talking between each other before calling it a night. Brad never really slept. His brain was racing and he was worried that he would sleep in and miss the morning run for food.

As soon as he heard the city coming to life Brad was up and out his door. He paced the hall for a while until he heard a sound coming from Iris' apartment. He took a big breath and knocked on the door. It was her father who answered.

"Good morning, Sir," said Brad nervously. "I have been sent to get food for my family and I was wondering if Iris might be able to help me pick the right things."

Iris' father looked at Brad with a wry smile.

"It is good to see a young man so motivated this early in the morning. Come in and sit down. She will join us soon."

Brad took a seat as Iris' father handed him a hot tea.

"You know that anybody down at the market would help you if you asked."

Brad sipped his tea before replying.

"Yes, sir," he said. "I am looking for a chance to spend some time alone with her. Just to talk. I think she might help me answer some questions."

"Alone, eh…."

Brad found himself sweating nervously.

"Oooooooh, what do we have here?" said Iris' mother as she entered the room. "Are you here to see my daughter young man?"

Brad blushed.

"Leave the poor boy alone, my love."

"We are giving you a bit of a hard time Brad, but I suspect that is what parents in all cultures do when a young man comes calling on their daughter."

Brad felt the heat in his face as he blushed even more.

"I trust your intentions, Brad.  Iris told us about you protecting your sisters yesterday. I only ask that you do the same for Iris."

"Yes, sir," said Brad, meaning what he said.

Iris' father stood up and gave Brad a good firm handshake, just as Iris entered the room.

"He needs a hand picking food. Go with him and find some for us as well."

"Yes, sir," said Iris.

"One more thing," said Iris' father, catching the two just before the door sealed behind them.  "We will be off to our tasks when you return.  You should spend the day with them again, so they don't get lost."

The door closed and as soon as it did, Iris leaned into Brad and whispered.

"Not sure if the was bold or brave, but my father respected it, which says a lot."

Brad's original plan was to pick Iris' brain during the brief trip shopping for food. With Iris being told by her father to spend the day with the MacIvers the pressure was off, and Brad enjoyed his time in the market. The trip took a little longer than planned. There were several Atlanteans who took some time away from what they were doing to introduce themselves.

"I wanted to meet you," said one. "We have not had visitors to our city for as long as I can remember. I also wanted to test my English. Is it good?

Brad shook their hand using the Atlantean handshake which he was finding he liked much more than the simple handshake he was used to.

"It is better than my own," said Brad.

Since he and Iris had left their building Brad had felt a sense of discomfort. As they moved through the streets and marketplace Brad was fairly confident he knew what was triggering that discomfort. As they were about to leave the market Brad decided to test his theory.

"Will I offend anyone if I talk to them?" he asked Iris quietly.

"No. Just introduce yourself first," said Iris.

Before she could ask why, Brad was introducing himself to someone. He shook their hand and asked them about the food in the bin in front of them. He then moved on to someone else and someone else, getting further away from Iris each time. As he went to greet a man, the man abruptly turned and walked away quickly, using the crowd to disappear. This confirmed Brad's suspicion. He turned to look back at Iris and noticed two men moving toward her. Brad quickly made his way back, taking Iris' arm as he stepped close beside her. He caught the eye of one of the men approaching her.

"The young woman is with me," he said firmly.

Iris was surprised at Brad's actions but quickly realized why he was doing it.

"Of course," said the man, who turned and walked away.

Brad looked over his shoulder and the second man had disappeared into the crowd as well.

The two walked back to their building without saying much. The entire time Brad was watching over his shoulder and carefully checking out everyone that walked past him. It wasn't until they were in the apartment that Brad relaxed. He quickly put the basket of food on the counter as the MacIvers gathered around the food, and then he asked Iris to come with him to his room.

"I can't do that," said Iris. "It wouldn't be proper."

Antonia overheard Iris and quickly assessed the situation.

"That is smart," said Antonia. "I think Brad just wants to talk away from the commotion out here. If I join you two, would that make it an acceptable social situation?"

"It would, thank you," said Iris.

There was no door in the room Brad was using as his own, but it was much quieter.

"I am sorry," said Brad. "I did not mean to offend you by asking you in here alone, or by what I did at the market."

Antonia looked at Brad curiously.

"Oh, you didn't," said Iris. It is a rule my parents have given me, and as you have seen there is probably a good reason for it. As for the market, your actions were seen as …"

Iris searched for the word.

"Honorable is what I think you would call it. I saw many around us nod in approval."

"Yes, but in doing so, I think I may have put you in danger."

Brad explained how he had only seen one person he thought was following them. He recognized him as someone that was always around Leonidis and the fact that he was not picking anything up from the market raised some red flags. When he avoided meeting him, Brad had confirmed his suspicion.

The man approaching Iris was much the same. Brad did not recognize him or the second man near her, but neither carried baskets and both were moving in a determined manner toward Iris.

"Are you okay," Antonia asked Iris.

"Yes. I didn't fully realize what was going on," she replied. "I thought Brad was doing what men commonly do in our culture and asserting that I belonged to him."

Brad blushed a deep red.

"I don't understand why you think you have put me in danger though."

"I do," said Antonia.

Antonia explained the plans Leonidis had laid out the day before to Brad, giving Brad a chance to collect himself from his embarrassment. She also summed up the conversation the MacIvers had the night before.

"I have to ask you if you think we might be right," said Antonia.

Iris took a few moments to collect her thoughts.

"Poor Diane," she said quietly as she thought about what Antonia had told her.

"Diane," questioned Brad.

Iris gave Brad a bit of a dirty look before it softened as she realized. "That man didn't even tell you his daughter's name, did he?"

Brad shook his head.

"Her name is Diane, and she is about to be wed to a man who she actually loves, which is not always the way," said Iris. "I suppose that is good because they can conceal the real reason for being with child. Her husband would probably never know. If she had the child out of wedlock she would be shunned."

"I didn't know," said Brad. "I wasn't going to do it anyway."

Iris sat quietly for a while. She began to shiver, and Antonia put her arm around you.

"If Leonidis didn't see me as an impediment to you having a child with his daughter before, he will definitely see it that way now that you claimed me as yours in the market. I am in danger," said Iris.

"I didn't…"

Antonia's foot shot out kicking Brad, stopping him from finishing what he was saying. She brushed a tear off Iris' cheek and motioned with her head for Brad to leave. As Brad stepped out of the door to his room, he found Allen sitting there.

"You okay, dude?"

"Yeah," said Brad quietly. "But I don't think Iris is."

"Give Toni and her some time. Come eat," said Allen.

Antonia didn't say anything. She let Iris work through what she was feeling. It was more than just being afraid.

"You are correct," said Iris.

"Before we talk about that, let's talk about Brad," said Antonia. "Brad has always been very protective of the people he cares for, and you are obviously one of those. I don't think he meant to claim you as his, but not because it isn't something he may want. It is because in our culture good men don't claim women as property. Brad is a good man."

"Yes, he is," said Iris.

"And as for your friend, Diane. Brad will never create a child with her. Which is why we are trying to find another way."

"That is good. There has been much speculation that Leonidis has been maneuvering to install himself as an emperor. Helen narrowly avoided being forced to marry his only son, but only because on his deathbed her father committed her to another man," said Iris.

The two young women sat at talked for a considerable time, about many things. When they came out of Brad's room, they found the rest of the MacIvers waiting quietly in the common area for them. Iris went directly to Brad and sat down beside him.

"Brad," said Antonia. "You claimed Iris as yours in the market. Iris understands what you did doesn't mean the same thing in our culture as it does hers but, to keep her protected you must continue to act as though you meant that claim."

Brad looked at Iris beside him.

"Are you okay with that?" he asked.

"Because you would ask that question, I am even more okay with that," said Iris. "Because you said those words in such a public place, it also means that Leonidis cannot allow you to be alone anywhere with his daughter."

"Sneaky," said Dawn.

"I like it," said Joane.

"Allen and I will explain things to Iris' parents," said Antonia.

"No," said Brad. "I need to do that myself. It is the proper thing to do."

Iris took hold of Brad's arm and squeezed it. Brad puffed up with pride.

"What about when we go home?" asked Deane. "Who protects Iris then?"

"We have not figured that out yet," said Antonia. "But you know how this family works. Iris is one of us now. A MacIver. We watch out for each other."

Antonia held her hand out and one by one each of the MacIvers stacked a hand on hers. They could all feel the same energy surge through them that they had the last time they did this. Sheila used her free hand to take hold of one of Iris' hands and add it to the pile. Iris felt a strange sensation overcome her as if all the stress and fear were washed out of her body.

# Chapter 7

The MacIvers had barely been gone from their apartment for more than a few minutes when a large group of Atlanteans swarmed the building carrying a variety of equipment. The MacIvers never saw this happen as they were on their way to where Iris' father was working. They were visiting the campus under the auspice of Bjorn wanting to show them art works in which the people looked very similar to Brad and maybe Brad would be able to see some of his ancestors. The real reason was that, with all of them there, they hoped to be able to create enough of a distraction that Allen would be able to access one of the computer terminals.

When they arrived at the campus, they found Helen waiting for them. This wasn't unexpected as Iris had arranged for a message to be delivered to her asking them to meet them. Helen walked past all of the MacIver and hugged Iris.

"Congratulations," said Helen. She continued speaking with Iris directly in their native language for a moment or two.

"I am hearing that we are the subject of much gossip in the city," said Iris as she took hold of Brad's arm.

"Yes, you are."

Brad recognized the voice as he turned his head towards it. Iris' father was standing there, a group of students behind him. Brad fought the urge to blurt out an explanation, but he could see that everyone was paying close attention, so he continued in the charade.

"Sir. I was not aware that this decision would get to you before I had an opportunity to discuss it with you," said Brad, trying to sound confident. "May I join you for dinner tonight so I can do this properly."

Iris' father stood with his arms crossed. He was a tall, lean man, but at the moment he had a very big presence. He looked carefully at his daughter who held his gaze, then back to Brad.

"You will join us for dinner, Brad. I trust your sisters will host Iris while you join us."

"Yes, sir. Thank you."

Iris' father walked away but every male in the hallway took a minute to shake Brad's hand and every female gave Iris a hug. When the hall had cleared Kelly spoke with Helen, asking her if it was possible to arrange a meeting with her and Leonidis, and some of the scientific leaders in the city to discuss options. Helen was a little reluctant, explaining that the city leaders would be the ones to make any decisions. Kelly convinced her that she understood that, but their process required them to hear all ideas before committing to one.

"It is the way our culture works," said Kelly.

It was clear that Helen wasn't completely falling for Kelly's pitch, but she agreed to make it happen.

"I would have suggested dinner, but it seems that Brad will be occupied," said Helen. "Well played."

Brad wasn't sure how to take those words. It could have been a congratulations or a subtle hint that Helen suspected something.

"We will host an evening event. We haven't had one of those in a long time," said Helen. "That way you can all attend."

Helen looked around as she spoke of all of them attending and realized Allen was not with the group.

"Where is your brother?"

The MacIvers looked around and realized Allen was not with them. They hadn't seen him slip away when everyone was distracted with Brad being confronted by Iris' father. Helen noticed that the MacIvers themselves seemed genuinely surprised that Allen wasn't with them, and she directed the people with her to look for him. Panic was starting to set in when Allen rolled off an elevator. He casually rolled up to join his family.

"Iris, what does a sign for a bathroom look like? I have been searching and searching. I don't know how many halls I have been down."

Iris pointed to a door right across from them.

"Oh," said Allen. "I am so used to looking for one that shows it will accommodate my wheelchair. Speaking of which," Allen said as he turned towards Helen. "I haven't seen anyone like me in the city. In a wheelchair or anything like it."

"I have not either," said Helen. "Not in my lifetime."

Allen casually pushed himself into the washroom.

"Perhaps if you spoke to our Doctor's Antonia, you might find a way to cure his deformity," said Helen.

"Different isn't deformed," exclaimed Bjorn. "There is nothing wrong with my brother."

Helen quickly apologized. It was a genuine apology, and the subject was dropped.

"I am off to view the inspection of the engine modules. Would you care to join me, Kelly?"

Kelly almost said an immediate yes, but she caught herself.

"I would like to, but Amar will have to join me if that is okay."

"Of course," said Helen.

When Allen returned, the MacIvers followed Bjorn to a large space that housed ancient art works. Antonia placed herself behind Allen's wheelchair and casually pushed him. It wasn't something she normally did as they all knew Allen liked to be independent, but Allen guessed why. He held his hands out and mimed tapping on a keyboard as he tipped his head back and looked up at his sister. Antonia just shook her head and when Allen laughed, she kneed the backside of his seat, which only made him laugh more.

The afternoon passed quickly, and the MacIvers enjoyed touring the artworks. They did come across paintings and statues that had a remarkable resemblance to Brad. They also noticed that they were now obviously being watched. The first man Brad had tried to greet in the market that morning was there, and not even making an effort to conceal that he was watching them. Brad responded by giving his arm to Iris and insisting she take it, then signing something to the others. The MacIvers recognized the signals because Brad had often used them when they were playing games. The group divided into three, one with Brad, one with Allen, and one with Bjorn, and they led their watchers off in several directions.

The kids took their time looking at the different displays, and if they saw one of the other groups, going intentionally in the opposite direction. They did nothing to hide from their watchers, but they were enjoying leading them around. When the lights dimmed, Iris suggested to Brad that it was time to leave and reminded him that he had a meeting with her parents.

"Marco," Brad called out loudly, surprising Iris and the watchers.

"Polo."

Brad heard "Polo" called out from two different directions. He and the others he was with made their way to the closest call where they found Bjorn, Sheila, and Deane.

"Marco," Brad called out again.

"Polo," came the callback from Allen, and quickly all the MacIvers were rejoined and made their way back to their apartment.

As they exited the campus they walked directly past the first man from the market. They were almost past the man when Brad turned suddenly, grabbing the man's forearm and shaking his hand vigorously.

"I am Brad. Thank you for keeping such a close eye on us today. We appreciate it."

The anger showed on the man's face as he shook Brad's hand.

"Caseus," said the man.

"Pleasure to meet you," said Brad, never taking his eyes off Caseus' face.

The handshake went on much longer than usual, as the two competed in a demonstration of grip strength, while not giving any indication to the others that was what was happening. When it became clear to Caseus that Brad was clearly stronger, he released his grip and walked away. Iris took Brad by the arm and moved him along and out of the building.

"There is brave and there is stupid, Brad," said Iris. "That was stupid."

"I completely agree," said Antonia.

Brad felt sufficiently chastised until he looked down and saw Allen hiding a thumbs-up so only Brad could see it.

When they arrived at their building, they were surprised to see everyone being stopped as they entered and put through a scanner. Iris' father had arrived a short time before them and when he saw the MacIvers and his daughter arrive he dropped back in the line so he could talk to them.

"They are saying some strange energy was traced to our building. It is gone now," Iris' father explained. "Probably nothing. Happens all the time."

"All the time," said Allen.

"We live in a sealed dome under an ocean. Anything and everything, like random energy spikes, that might compromise that are carefully monitored and investigated."

There wasn't much of a delay. Every person walked through a scanner and they weren't held up after that. The MacIvers got past the scanner just as easily, except for Allen. His wheelchair would not fit through the scanner, nor was it permitted. Allen was held back while the Atlanteans discussed what to do. It wasn't a situation they had every dealt with, and they had strict protocols on the process. Luckily Helen was just leaving the building after bringing Kelley and Amar back. She noticed the commotion and intervened.

"Did anyone else show any signs of it," Allen heard Helen as the workers who responded negatively.

"Okay then. They have been together all day, so logically if he had been exposed, they would. Run a handheld device over him, and if anyone questions you, send them to me."

Allen was quickly allowed past the barrier after that.

# Chapter 8

It was a girls' evening in the MacIver's apartment. Allen, Bjorn, and Amar retreated to the deck while Iris helped the MacIver girls get dressed and do their hair in current Atlantean fashion in preparation for the event they would be attending that night. Brad was across the hall meeting with Iris' parents.

Bjorn worked at a sketch of the city skyline while he sat on the deck. Amar idly chatted with him, looking up often as some fascinating creature swam outside the dome nearby. Allen was quiet. Bjorn and Amar just figured that Allen was thinking, or perhaps deciphering the computer code he had seen earlier. They were quite impressed at how quickly and easily Allen had slipped away from them at the campus, using the opportunity to access one of the computer terminals.

"It wasn't that hard," said Allen when they had asked them about it. "Nobody wants to see the boy in the wheelchair. Especially when there is only one."

Inside the girls were laughing and giggling as they tried on clothes that Iris and her mother and brought over. Leonidis had sent over some clothing that had been waiting for them when the got home, but the girls only had to take one look at those clothes before rejecting them. If there was one thing that their mother had taught the MacIver girls, it was how to be strong independent women, with pride in their appearance no matter how others viewed them. None of the MacIver girls saw any need to expose as much skin as the clothing Leonidis had sent them would show.

"He wants to display us like trophies," said Joane. "For all the other men to see. Are all Atlantean men pedophiles?"

"Pedophiles?" asked Iris, not understanding the word.

"People that have a sexual attraction to children," explained Antonia.

"Oh," said Iris "We have different words for that, but no. It is frowned upon. But if you are a man of a higher caste or one of the Three as Leonidis is, the rules don't always apply the same."

Across the hall Brad sat at a table, Iris' mother and father sitting directly across from him. Neither looked happy.

"What have you done to my daughter?" demanded Iris' mother.

Brad was taken aback by the question.

"Nothing. I haven't touched her in any inappropriate way," exclaimed Brad, panic setting in.

"No son. I think you misunderstand," said Iris' father. "In our culture, to claim a woman is a lifetime commitment from the woman. It makes her unavailable to any others. Forever. No matter what the man does or what happens to him. And we assume you are leaving at some point."

Brad apologized. He went into every little detail about what had happened at the market that morning and why he had done it and said the words he did. He could see that Iris' parents were starting to understand, but he knew they did not have enough information to fully comprehend what had happened.

"Sir. Mam. Your daughter is amazing, and I trust her implicitly. She is like that because of you, I am sure, so I am going to extend that trust to you," said Brad.

Brad explained about his meeting with Leonidis and Leonidis' plan for his daughter to have Brad's baby. He told Iris' parents what they had pieced together, and why, even though Brad had not meant the words he said in the market in the Atlantean sense, he and the others felt it would be better to act as though he had. As Brad explained these things to Iris' parents, he could see their looks and demeanor change. He could see they too understood that their daughter was in danger.

Iris' father got up from the table, retrieved two cups of tea, and set one down in front of Brad before he sat down himself. Brad could see the wheels turning in his head.

"Brad, I thank you for asking for my permission to claim my daughter as your own before you left for the market this morning," said Iris' father. "I only wish you would not have let your excitement overtake you and that you would have saved making that claim until this evening, as we had planned."

Iris' father spoke the last four words very slowly and clearly. Brad got the message. This was the story that they would tell everyone.

"What about when Brad leaves us? Iris will still be in danger. Probably more than she is now," said Iris' mother.

Brad had already thought about this. He had even pulled aside Allen at one point as talked to him about it.

"There are two options," said Brad. "I stay, but that has many more problems than it solves, and I am not sure anyone would be any safer."

Iris' father nodded in agreement. Brad took a deep breath before continuing.

"So, if you would allow it, Iris could return home with us."

Iris' mother raised an eyebrow.

"Not like that," said Brad quickly. "My family is not like most. We are a family that came together by chance. Our parents are wonderful, and I know they would take Iris in as one of the family. A sister to me. And she would have her own choices in the future. Not be claimed."

Brad could see tears welling up in Iris' mother's eyes as she got up and left the room.

"I am sorry," said Brad. "It is the only solution I can think of that will keep her safe. You have my word that I will always be there to protect her."

Iris's father got up and shook Brad's hand, griping Brad's forearm with both his hands.

"That I do not doubt. Nor do I doubt your parents because I can see them in the man in front of me as you saw us in Iris."

"Thank you, sir," said Brad.

Iris' father reached into a box on the table and pulled out two nearly identical bracelets, just as her mother returned to the room.

"I picked these up on my return home today," she said. "They indicate that you and my daughter are one, even when apart. There is a biological marker in them so you must take this one," she said, handing Brad the heavier of the two bracelets, and returning the second to its box before handing it to Brad. "This one you must place on Iris' wrist yourself."

Iris' mother hugged Brad.

"Welcome to the family, son."

"I am proud to call a good man like you my son," said Iris' father as he shook Brad's hand one more time. "Now, I will make a big show of this as I walk you across the hall.

We have our privacy in here. It the halls we don't."

Brad nodded.

"Play along but know this," said Iris' father seriously. "What we do in the hall is a necessary act, but what we have said in here is not. You are part of our family now."

Iris' father walked Brad across the hall, loudly calling him son and laughing. As the door to the MacIver's apartment opened, he called loudly for his daughter who quickly came to him.

Iris' father pushed Brad forward.

"Give it to her son," he said loudly. "Before I change my mind."

Brad opened the box in his hand and pulled out the bracelet. Iris looked at the bracelet, and then at her father, noticing that her mother was standing behind him. Her mother nodded and Iris extended her left hand. Brad slipped the bracelet over Iris' wrist and felt it vibrate as it locked in place. Iris nodded shyly at Brad.

"I would have preferred that he not have been so impatient and waited until supper as we planned," proclaimed Iris' father loudly as he stood in the doorway so the door would not close. "But it is done now. I have a new son. I trust you girls will see that my daughter's purity is preserved until the ceremony in 30 days, as is our tradition."

With those words, Iris' father grabbed his wife and they returned across the hall.

"Ummmm, what just happened?" asked Amar who had walked into the common area half way through the scene.

"What just happened!" exclaimed Antonia. "How about what the…"

"Don't you dare," said Kelly firmly.

"Heck," said Antonia. "What the heck?"

Brad motioned for everyone to sit down. Iris remained standing beside him and as Brad started to tell her to sit down, she shook her head. Brad quickly understood that that was what would be expected of her.

"It is real. It is official," said Brad, holding up his left arm and showing the bracelet on his wrist.

"I had to do it to keep Iris safe."

Brad noticed Iris flinch a little as he said that. He turned to face her as he spoke.

"I am happy that it has turned out this way," said Brad. "It wasn't forced on me. It was my idea. My choice."

Iris smiled shyly.

"So, you are staying?" asked Sheila.

Brad shook his head.

"So, you are going to love her and leave her," said Kelly.

Iris started to respond, but Brad spoke first.

"Trust you to be straight to the point," said Brad as he looked at Kelly. "No. Iris will be coming home with us. One way or another, she is a MacIver now."

"Well, this will take some explaining to Mom and Dad," said Amar.

"I am sure we all want to hear all the details," said Allen, interrupting the conversation. "But we have some place to be and we have to get going."

The MacIvers filed out the door, meeting up with Iris' parents in the hall who were also attending the evening event. Brad waited for everyone to leave, holding Iris back with him. When the door closed, he turned and spoke to her.

"I am sorry," he said. "I am sure this is not what you wanted, and I know that this is a lifetime commitment you were forced into, but I put you at risk and I need you to be safe."

Iris looked deep into Brad's eyes, then leaned in and kissed him gently on the cheek.

"Do not be sorry. I am happy."

# Chapter 9

"Welcome. Welcome," said Leonidis, eagerly greeting Brad as he entered what appeared to be a ballroom.

As Leonidis shook Brad's hand, Iris saw him carefully looking at Brad's left wrist. Iris wrapped her arm in Brad's, taking care to make sure her Bracelet was easily seen by Leonidis.

"Yes, well…I guess congratulations are in order," said Leonidis haughtily.

"Thank you," said Iris demurely, keeping her eyes down.

Leonidis walked away quickly, making a point of finding somebody else to greet.

"That was subtle," whispered Brad to Iris.

Iris giggled.

"You cannot expect a girl to be subtle about being claimed. That would be insulting to you."

"Maybe," said Brad. "But I think you took pleasure in doing that to him."

Iris only giggled a little more.

Sheila was the next MacIver to be greeted by Leonidis. Allen watched from close by as Leonidis looked Sheila over up and down, then did the same to Deane and Joane.

"Did the clothes I sent you not arrive?" Leonidis asked he looked over his shoulder at a man who seemed to be his assistant.

"They did," said Sheila. "I hope you understand that in our society it would be inappropriate for children like us to dress so revealingly for an event like this."

Sheila had made a point of speaking quite loudly so others around her. Leonidis went red in the face, and he started to raise his hand, but Amar stepped in extending his arm for a handshake. This forced Leonidis to return the handshake as other Atlanteans looked on. He almost stomped away to the front of the room as someone asked everyone to find a seat. When the room was quiet Helen stood up and addressed the room.

She welcomed the MacIvers, each by their name. This was followed by an explanation of what the MacIvers were there for and where they came from, though that information seemed common knowledge among Atlanteans now. She also explained that, while they likely found it unusual, it was common practice for the MacIver's people to invite all people to speak before they make any major plans.

The last comment started a roll of whispered conversation throughout the room. Helen continued.

"Before we hear any other ideas, perhaps we should hear from Leonidis, who as one of the Three has already come up with some ideas. We do owe him our thanks for the foresight in reaching out past the ice, and in finding help," said Helen.

There was a thunder in the room as people stomped their feet on the floor. Leonidis stood, lifting his hand, but never removing his eyes from Brad.

"Thank you," said Leonidis. "I believe my plan is already well in the works. With the union of Brad and Iris, I suspect that Brad has chosen to remain among us. That would make him one of the Three and would allow for us to relocate."

This was one of the scenarios that the MacIvers had discussed, although when they discussed it, they did not consider that Brad would be officially in a union with an Atlantean. They had no idea how they were going to argue against it other than Brad needed to return home. Turns out they didn't have to.

"May I speak?"

Antonia recognized the doctor she had spent the day with. Leonidis hesitated but Helen boldly stepped in.

"Please do," said Helen. "I believe that is why our guests have asked us here."

"We already know that the young man's genetics are not pure enough on their own. They need to be mixed with pure Atlantean," said the doctor. He was about to continue but saw the stare Leonidis was giving him.

This was information that Helen had not been provided, though from the looks exchanged between Leonidis and the Doctor, it wasn't new information. Helen acted as if she were aware of this already.

"Thank you for reminding us," said Helen.

"The boy needs to become a man and make his own boy," called out a random voice in the room. His comment was cheered by the men in the room and both Brad and Iris blushed.

Another man stood up and waited for the room to quiet.

"I support the last comment, but it doesn't meet the deadline we need to launch."

"We can speed the pregnancy up," said one woman. "We do it all the time for new workers or when we have pandemics."

The Doctor rose again, avoiding Leonidis' look.

"When we do that, we alter genetics," said the doctor. "We could be eliminating the solution in the process."

Brad found himself sweating. The MacIvers had talked about these ideas coming up, but Brad wasn't sure if he was sweating at the thought of staying or all the talk of a baby. Iris noticed the beads of sweat on his forehead. She casually leaned over and gave Brad a gentle kiss on the cheek, wiping his forehead as she did. She wasn't even sure Brad had noticed the wipe of his forehead, but he did relax at the kiss.

"We have less than 10 days to launch if we are to break through the ice and enter the right orbit to return us home," said a voice near the front.

The room filled with the sound of mumbling as the Atlanteans talked amongst themselves. A large man standing at the back of the room added his voice to the conversation.

"Why do we have to leave? They are coming here to our home. We can just destroy them when they land."

Brad watched Leonidis smile at this statement.

Allen tried to get the attention of the Atlanteans a couple of times. It was Iris' father that spoke up and got the attention of the room.

"I believe our guest has something to say."

Allen rolled himself out of the crowd to the front of the room.

"May I speak, Helen?" asked Allen.

Helen nodded and motioned for those standing in the room to sit down.

"You are right, sir," said Allen. "You could easily destroy the ships that will land here, but as your own history tells you, the people of Earth are quick to fight. Those few ships would soon be followed by many more equipped for death."

Allen paused for dramatic effect, to let those words set in.

"Is there anyone here whose task is programming the computers that control certain aspects of this city?"

A young man stood up.

"What if I could help you reprogram the base code that determines what genetics are needed to run your ship?" asked Allen.

The young man shook his head.

"The knowledge to change that code was lost to us long ago," he said. "Ancient texts tell us that the race that helped create this ship, refused to provide us with the ability to change those protocols. The symbol over the controls says specifically 'so one doesn't rule all.'"

This was new information to Allen and the MacIvers. It was also information that was triggering to Leonidis who spoke out angrily.

"I don't understand this process. It is not our way. It is getting us nowhere."

Allen continued.

"I should take a moment to tell you about my family," said Allen to the room. "As you can see, we all come from different backgrounds, and we all have different skills, which is why, when we were called here it was all of us and not just Brad."

Allen motioned for Brad to join him at the front.

"Brad is not only an Atlantean descendent, but also a fearless leader, a builder, a protector, and a warrior," said Allen hyping his brother up and getting the response from the men in the room that he hoped for.

"Antonia is a healer. Kelly is an engineer. Joane has an ability with languages. Deane, geology. Sheila can read people and creatures. Bjorn, as some of you have seen see things more clearly than others."

Allen paused again. He could say more. He knew more about each of his brothers and sisters, but it was for them to discover.

"I could keep going, but we are like you in that we all work together and compliment each other's skills, so we are able to accomplish great things together. I am the mathematician and coder among us. So, if you would consider letting us look at that programming, the MacIvers will do whatever it takes to get you away safely to your next destination."

"If the Three will allow it, I have no objection."

"I like the idea," said the Doctor.

Others in the room called out their voice of support. Helen stood up and held up her hand until the room was silent.

"I will support that," said Helen. "What say you, Leonidis?"

Leonidis looked so angry that those in his vicinity had moved away from him.

"I will agree, but you will be monitored to insure there are no changes made without my permission.

Allen turned to face Leonidis. He bowed his head and said thank you.

"What happens to us when the ship leaves?

Sheila turned to where the voice came from and saw a group of women and children. There was something about them that didn't sit right with her. It wasn't the first time she had this type of feeling, but Allen's words about her emboldened her. Leonidis and her both started to speak at the same time. Leonidis slammed his fist down on the table, but Sheila continued.

"We will come and speak with you tomorrow," said Sheila as she pointed at herself, Deane, and Amar.

There was some commotion as Leonidis stepped forward towards the crowd. Instinctively Brad stepped forward as well catching Leonidis' attention.

"We can talk about your concerns and see how we can help."

Leonidis turned on his heels and quickly left the room.

"I believe we have accomplished a lot here this evening," said Helen. "Return to your homes. Another day comes soon."

The crowd quickly dispersed leaving the MacIvers and Helen alone in the big space.

"Do you think you can," Helen asked Allen."

"I will know when I see the code," said Allen.

Helen looked around the room, then at the MacIvers, which now included Iris.

"We called for your help and brought you into a dangerous game apparently. Be safe."

# Chapter 10

"Geology?" Deane asked Allen.

"And geography".

"How do you figure?" asked Deane.

Allen explained to his sister how he had watched her over the years. He pointed out how she always knew these odd facts and how during their first day on Europa, she was the one who was able to identify locations on the old map of Earth that none of them recognized. There were other reasons Allen knew, but he wasn't about to share them.

"Not saying you are wrong, but it's not really anything special," said Deane.

"We shall see," said Allen.

The MacIvers sat around chatting. They were pleased with how the meeting had gone, and after observing Leonidis' reactions, they were sure the public meeting had been the right way to go.

"You know what my favorite part was?" asked Amar.

The others waited for him to tell them.

"Warrior…" Amar said in an exaggerated tone as he punched Brad in the shoulder.

The MacIvers laughed together, loudly.

"That was a little dramatic," said Antonia.

Allen shrugged his shoulders.

"I thought we could benefit from Leonidis and his henchmen having a little bit of fear," said Allen. "Anyway, I am exhausted. I am going to call it a day."

It had been a long day for everyone, and they were all ready for bed.

"Am I supposed to walk you home now," Brad asked Iris.

Iris squeezed his arm and laughed.

"I am your family now. I stay here."

"Ugh…Ugh…Ugh…" Brad stammered.

Iris laughed at his discomfort as she got up from beside him and joined Antonia.

"You are safe Brad," said Antonia. "For 30 days she is the responsibility of the girls in the family. Then she is all yours."

Brad looked uncomfortable and all the girls in the room laughed at him trying to come up with some words. They had all left for their rooms before Brad found his tongue. There was an extra sleeping pad in Antonia's room which she Iris guessed her father had brought over before they returned home.

Allen didn't go to bed, as tired as he was. Instead, he sat out on the deck, watching the dome above him as the bioluminescent life moved outside it. It reminded him of a saltwater aquarium that sat in a dark corner at the local Chinese food restaurant they went to on occasion. He started to nod off when he realized Sheila was sitting on the deck with him.

"What are you not telling us, Allen?"

Allen looked at his sister knowing he would have to carefully navigate this conversation.

"A lot," he said, being completely honest. "But if you can be more specific, maybe I can tell you more."

Allen always had his secrets. It didn't take Sheila's senses to read that. All the MacIvers know, and they let him have them.

"About the computer code."

"Ah…It is not if I can change the code, but what do I

change it to?" said Allen quietly.

"There is more going on in this city than we are seeing, Shelia. But you already sense that."

Sheila nodded her head.

"We only have a few short days left. Do I change the code to pick the leaders Leonidis tells me to? Do I change it so it needs no genetic code? Do I do something else?"

Sheila didn't answer right away. She didn't answer at all.

"You should go to bed to sleep, Allen."

"I will, but I need to ask you to do one thing for me," said Allen.

Sheila waited.

"Whether she comes with us, or stays behind, Iris is going to be hurt by a loss. I need to know which is the worse option," said Allen.

Sheila tilted her head to the right, which was something she did naturally when she was concentrating on reading a person.

"I don't know what you are thinking, Allen MacIver. I do know that Brad will give up everything to protect her. He maybe doesn't understand real love yet, but he has a sense of honor and duty that he might as well be married to her already."

"That's our warrior," said Allen, trying to add some levity to the moment.

Sheila laughed lightly and went to bed. Allen found his way to bed as well.

———————————————

Brad woke to knock sounds. He tried to ignore it, but it persisted. It took him a moment or two to orient himself and when his eyes found the door he saw Iris there. He quickly jumped up from his bed mat.

"Is everything okay?"

"It won't be if we don't get to market and get food for Mom and Dad and the rest of you."

"I'll be out in a second."

Brad quickly changed his clothes and made up his room the way Iris had shown them. He stumbled as he walked into the common space. Iris handed him two baskets and they headed for the door.

"Where is everyone else," asked Brad as he left the apartment.

"Still sleeping," said Iris, laughing. "You have two families now as the elder son. Your day starts earlier."

Brad had a smart mouth response on the tip of his tongue, but he thought twice before saying it.

The two of them made their way to the market quickly, and through the market without any excitement. There did not seem to be any watchers today, but Brad did notice men giving them a wide berth as they walked through the market and down the street.

"Warrior is a strong word in our culture," whispered Iris when Brad looked at her questionably.

Now Brad understood why they were being given a wide berth. Allen's dramatics might have been too effective.

Back at the apartment, they stopped by Iris' apartment first. Her father was sitting on their deck drinking his tea. He nodded his head in acknowledgment as Iris set down a basket but didn't say anything. When they entered the MacIver apartment, they found it silent still. Iris set the food basket down and took Brad out to the deck where she sat him down. She disappeared briefly back inside the apartment before returning with a hot tea for Brad and an electronic tablet.

Brad sipped eagerly on the tea.

"You know I was going to complain earlier," said Brad. "But I could get used to this."

"You wouldn't dare complain," said Iris laughing, reminding Brad how much he liked her smile.

Iris handed the tablet to Brad and showed him how to work it.

"You should read this section," said Iris. "It is about

the protocols you and I are expected to follow in public now. People will be judging. Enjoy your tea."

Iris disappeared back into the house where she prepared breakfast for the MacIvers. Once they were all up, they had a quiet breakfast and made their plans for the day. Allen was going to try and find the computer guy to get a look at the code. He asked for Kelly and Joane to join him. Sheila asked Iris where she would find that woman from the end of the meeting last night and Iris bristled a little.

"You will not find them here. They are in one of the separate pods. They are women who have lost their husbands or had children out of union, and men who do not fit in with the norms of our society," said Iris.

"I knew this city was too perfect," said Sheila angrily. "So, when she said 'when the ship leaves' she meant when they get left behind."

"Yes," said Iris. "My parents tell me it was never like that in the past, but it was a decision from the Three."

"So…," said Bjorn. "If Brad left you, that would happen to you."

Iris nodded. Brad felt a wave of anger inside him.

"I don't care what Mom or Dad says," said Bjorn. "You are coming home with us."

Iris reached out and hugged Bjorn.

"Nobody gets left behind," said Allen. "I won't fix

anything if they are not brought into this city."

"Leonidis will not approve," said Iris.

"Can you bring us to them, Iris?" asked Brad. "Allen, Kelly, and Joe have their own thing to do, but we need to talk to these people. Nobody gets left behind."

Iris explained to the MacIvers about the transportation corridor under the sea floor. She had never used it, but she knew it was there. She cautioned the MacIvers because there were men there like the big guy at the meeting who wanted to destroy the ships when they arrived. There was also much illness there. None of this changed the resolve of the MacIvers to meet with them.

The bell rang and Iris answered the door. Helen was standing there with the computer guy from the night before.

"We thought it best to get an early start," said Helen. "I trust that is okay."

"Of course," replied Allen. "Kelly and Jo will be joining us."

"That will be fine. May I ask what the others have planned for the day?"

Iris slipped into Atlantean as she talked to Helen.

"Well then," said Helen returning to English. "You had best be on your way before the opportunity is no longer there."

They MacIvers got the hint and followed Allen out the door. The split into their two groups and went their separate ways outside the building. Antonia insisted that they make a stop at the medical center first where she found the doctor she had accompanied on his rounds. She explained to the doctor about where they were going and asked for any medical supplies that he could provide that she might be able to use. The doctor gave her a basket of supplies, and masks for each of them, warning Antonia to be careful.

Iris led the MacIvers around the outside edge of the city, then down to a chamber below the ocean floor. There they waited for one of the transportation vehicles to come by. As they were waiting three more people joined them, each of them carrying a large pack and wearing a mask. It took a minute for Antonia to recognize the Doctor. Iris was just as surprised to see them.

"We cannot go to the pod to treat those that are there," said the doctor. "But you are guests of the Atlanteans, and we must act appropriately to keep you safe."

Antonia caught a little wink from the doctor and she understood.

"Best mask up now. There are infectious diseases there and weakened immunity because some are sick. We don't want to make things worse."

The MacIvers put on the medical masks and boarded the transit car as it pulled up. It wasn't a long ride to the other end of the tunnel, but it was a bit of a claustrophobic experience. The tunnel was poorly lit, and the walls were not even an arm's length away.  When they arrived at the pod, they were surprised to find people waiting for them.  At the front of the line was the big guy from the previous night. Brad walked up and shook his hand.

"You are huge," said Brad as he tipped his head back to look at the man in front of him.

The man laughed a big belly laugh which turned into a hacking cough. Antonia started to step forward to help the big man, but one of the doctors stopped her.

"We are going to set up here," said the doctor.  "Take a seat, John."

The doctor opened his pack and pulled out some equipment and medication.  He quickly checked the big guy over and gave him a bottle of the medication.

"We have seen John before," said the doctor treating John.  The other two doctors had already set up as well and were calling people over to be cared for.

"He was deemed to be too large a drain on the city's resources because his persistent lung infection prevented him from doing any heavy work."

"That's what your records say," said John.  "I got kicked out because old Leo boy there wanted me to be one of his henchmen and I said no."

Brad looked at the doctor and the doctor nodded.

"Yup.  Even offered me a chance to come back if I

bashed you around a bit last night. Like I am going to fight some warrior," said John. "I can barely even breathe."

"You would have won that battle I think," said Brad. "Can I ask why you didn't?"

John pointed at Sheila.

"These are good people here. Just bad situations," said John. "She talked to my friend like she was any other person. Didn't let old Leo boy shut her up. Your sister saved your warrior ass."

John laughed deeply again which brought on another coughing fit.

"And I called it right," said John after catching his breath. "You kept your word. Came to us to talk to us. And brought the good docs with you."

John got up and as he walked past Brad he slapped Brad on the shoulder.

"You're a good man. Good people. I will go get the others."

Neither the MacIvers nor the doctors had to go any further into the pod. Everyone came to them. Antonia helped treat those who were sick. There were so many though that they ran out of medications before the day was half over. Despite that the doctors still examined everyone, writing down the medications they should take if they could find them.

Sheila, Deane, and Amar made sure they spoke to every person. Brad stood watch for trouble. He did what Iris had told him, but he saw nothing but kind people in need. Iris translated for many of the Atlanteans who never had the opportunity to learn English like those in the city. As the day wore on, she too realized that the stories she had heard in the city were far from the truth.

# Chapter 11

Kelly explained what everything was as they made their way through the Aqua Nexus. Helen was amazed at how much Kelly had retained from their short tour. They made their way to what appeared to be a computer lab and as they entered, all but one person cleared out of the room. The man accompanying them spoke in Atlantean and the person who had remained in the room brought up some computer code on a big screen.

"This is part of the code. Can you tell us anything about it?"

Allen looked over the code. It was not in English, or any language he was familiar with, but he was able to quickly pick out repeating patterns and decipher that this code opened and closed some switches and the inputs that triggered those actions. Kelly whispered something in Allen's ear, and he laughed.

"May I have a pen and paper," asked Allen.

Allen quickly drew a sketch of what the code told him was happening.  He showed it to Kelly.

"Water valves," said Kelly.

The Atlanteans in the room looked surprised when Kelly said those words.

Allen turned his wheelchair so he could face the computer guy who had come with Helen.

"Caleb, right?" said Allen.  "Kelly tells me that is what this other man called you."

The man nodded.

"Well Caleb, this code opens and closes some switches which operate some valves.  This is the order the switches are triggered," said Allen as he handed over the piece of paper he had sketched on.  "Kelly tells me that would likely be water control valves."

"So that's what that does," said Caleb.  "Thank you for figuring it out for us."

Allen started to roll himself towards the door.

"Sorry Caleb," said Allen "But if you were unable to decipher your own, what is obviously modern code, then you are wasting my time. We should go Helen."

The man at the computer keyboard made a slight choking sound and Allen knew his sister was right.

"I am sorry," said Caleb.  "We had to test you."

Allen stopped. He turned his wheelchair slowly around. Caleb quickly motioned to the other man to bring up another page of code. Allen looked it over then motioned to his sisters to follow him as he once again headed towards the door, this time his sisters following.

"Stop," sad Helen firmly. "What is going on here?"

"It would seem he is unable to interpret the old code, just as we are."

Allen was part way out the door, but he stopped, backed in, and turned around.

"Helen, are these other men outside the door with you?" asked Allen.

Hellen nodded.

"Okay. So here is what is really happening. Caleb, who seemed keen to help us last night, has had a sheet of gibberish put up on the screen that means and does nothing, and he is trying to convince you not to let me see more."

Helen called to the men outside the door, and they stepped inside the room.

"Is what Allen is saying accurate," asked Helen.

Caleb started to speak, but Helen held up her hand to stop him.

"Not you. Him," she said as she looked at the man behind the keyboard.

"It is just a bunch of random characters strung together as I was instructed to do," said the man.

Helen said something in Atlantean and Caleb reluctantly left the room with Helen's two men accompanying him. Helen then pointed at the keyboard silently. The man quickly brought up another sheet of code.

Allen positioned himself at a desk so he could get a better view of the code. He motioned for his sisters to pull up a chair beside him. He took his time reading it, finding the patterns and the math. He pulled out the pen and paper he was given earlier and made notes.

"I take it this is the real thing," said Helen as she found herself a chair.

"It is," said Allen.

"Well, that is a good thing for someone," Helen said quietly as she looked at the man at the keyboard.

"Can I see more?" asked Allen.

"More?" the man asked. "That is all we have. All that we have been able to access."

Allen looked at Helen. Helen looked at the man. The man looked back, the fear showing in his eyes.

"This code only changes the direction of the ship," said Allen.

"If there is more, I don't know where to find it."

"I do," said Kelly. "We need to see the sun."

"That is cryptic, said Joane.

"Not really," said Helen as she turned toward the man at the keyboard. "Go home and be glad you have a forgettable face."

He didn't have to be asked twice to leave. Helen guided the other three up to the top floor of the Nexus and Kelly led them to the control room.

"You will have to activate your section," said Kelly.

Helen turned and looked out the dome, watching the eddies of water. She pointed at a creature that had attached itself to the clear dome, tapping against the inside of the dome-like someone would tap on the side of an aquarium, trying to get the attention of the creatures on the other side.

"Fascinating animals," said Helen. "I have held them in my bare hand. They are soft and if you touch them right, they vibrate ever so gently. Sometimes we will find them in a group on the side of the dome and together they will hum. You can hear it inside, which is amazing when you consider how thick this structure is."

Helen placed a finger against the dome directly in front of the creature adding some perspective to what the MacIvers were seeing. The dome that appeared to be almost non-existent without that perspective could now be seen to be an arm's length deep. Allen rolled up beside Helen to try and get a closer look at the creature she was admiring, but from his seated position, he could not see much better.

Helen looked down at him.

"Can you not stand at all?"

"No," said Allen.

"Did you have an accident?"

"I have never walked," said Allen.

"And yet you are an amazing brilliant young man. Nothing seems to stop you," Helen commented. "And if there is something you can't do?"

"He finds a way," said Kelly. "And we support him in whatever way he asks."

"Fascinating," said Helen, as she returned to looking at the creature.

Allen wasn't sure how to interpret what Helen had just said. It wasn't unusual for people to ask what he was able to do, or just assume he couldn't do much of anything. He was not used to adults asking about why he was in a wheelchair, though it wasn't unusual for others his age and younger to ask him about it. He looked back at Kelly and Joane who both just shrugged their shoulders.

"That's a female," said Helen. "As beautiful and soft and gentle as they are, when they are threatened, usually by a male of their species, those flowing, feather-like hairs, become stiff, razor-edged blades. If it is just one, she will sit there, daring the male to attack. If she has children nearby, she will launch a vicious assault to protect those children, even if it costs her life. When food and resources become scarce, the females will gather together, extend those blades, and move slowly forward into a new area, chasing out other animals that may be a threat to them or their children."

Helen turned to Allen again, this time getting down on one knee. She took hold of one of Allen's thighs and ran her hands down his leg, doing the same with his other leg. Allen stiffened in shock and surprise.

"When I told you we have nobody like you in Atlantis, I was being honest with you," said Helen. "But that is only because in recent generations, children that don't meet our standards of normality are not allowed to continue life."

"Oh my God!," exclaimed Joane, quickly putting her hand over her mouth to contain her shock and anger.

Kelly placed herself next to Allen, ready for something to happen. Helen stood up slowly. She pointed at the pod far below them outside the dome.

"Your family will meet many of the mothers of those children today."

Allen began to understand what Helen was telling them. He resisted the urge to interrupt her, and his sisters followed his lead. Helen returned once again to observing the creature. Her head swayed slightly, in sync with the feather-like hairs of the creature moving with the water current.
She played with a bracelet on her left wrist. Allen had noticed it before, but now he recognized it for what it was, a symbol of a union, like the ones Brad and Iris now wore.

"I would be over there if I were not one of the Three," said Helen very quietly. "Instead, my husband is there. He was a giant of man but had a heart that purred like one of those."

Allen now understood Helen's reverie. Kelly walked up beside Helen and placed herself close. Helen extended her arm around Kelly's shoulders.

"You are a remarkable young woman, Kelly MacIver," said Helen. "All the young women in your family are."

Helen gave Kelly a firm squeeze, then collected herself.

"Come. Let's see if we can get you access to that code.

Helen sat in her chair and the wall of panels came to life. Allen's eyes opened wide with excitement. He looked over the screens, occasionally asking Helen what a symbol meant. When he identified one screen as a control panel he began tapping away. He spent long periods just staring at the screens, now and then asking Joane what she thought a symbol could mean. He called Kelly over at one point and spoke quietly to her.

"You are not making any changes, are you?" asked Helen.

"No," said Allen. "I need access to the other terminal to do that. It seems like any changes have to be entered on more than one terminal to be accepted."

"That is good."

Leonidis' voice startled everyone in the room. He seemed to take pleasure in that.

"I did not want to interrupt your work," said Leonidis as he approached the terminal Allen was working at. "You seem to have got much further than my people have."

Leonidis looked over the screens, shaking his head.

"You understand this?"

"I think so," said Allen cautiously. "There is a lot of code there."

Leonidis walked over to one of the empty chairs and sat down in it. The arms of the chair wrapped around his forearms and the wall of screens opposite him lit up.

"Is this one any different?"

Allen rolled over to the new set of screens. Within moments he had brought up the same code that he was looking at on Helen's screens. He rolled himself back so he could see both walls of panels clearly, and compared them.

"They are identical," said Allen.

Leonidis was making the same comparison of the screens, but Allen could see he was doing it a few characters at a time. He eventually gave up on his comparison, his eyes lost in the code.

"How do we get access to the third station to make these changes," asked Leonidis. "I assume changes have to be made at all three."

Allen was careful to choose his words.

"It seems that way. I need some time to think this through."

"Fine," said Leonidis, sounding frustrated.

Leonidis attempted to stand up quickly, but he was held back by the gauntlet that shrouded his forearms. He sat back even more frustrated and tugged at his arms. He then closed his eyes and took a deep breath and the shrouds around his arms retracted into the chair.

"You will tell me before accessing anything in this room in the future," he said firmly. "I am not even sure why you were permitted access in the first place," Leonidis added, giving Helen a very dirty look.

"They are not Atlanteans, and this is why they are here," said Helen firmly.

Leonidis stormed away and Helen muttered something in Atlantean.

"I don't think we want that translated," said Joane.

Helen looked at Joane with a wry smile.

"You do not, child."

# Chapter 12

Helen left Allen, Joane, and Kelly once exiting the Aqua Nexus. She told them she was confident they could make their own way back to their apartment and didn't give them a chance to object. A few minutes into their walk they came across the rest of their family who had just returned from the pod. Allen noticed how exhausted they all looked. Even Joane commented on how they looked like they had a rough day.

"That could be because the air is not the same quality in the pod that it is here."

Antonia was surprised to hear this, but it explained why she felt so drained.

"This is one of the doctors that…"

Kelly paused, remembering the justification the doctor had used in the morning.

"That traveled with us to make sure we did not suffer any ill effects of being exposed to those people."

Joane looked at her sister through squinted eyes, very disapprovingly. Allen understood the reason for Antonia's harsh words as he watched other people walk past them. He rolled up and shook the doctor's hand.

"Thank you for watching out for them," said Allen. "May I ask you a question?"

"Of course," replied the doctor.

"Are there any differences physically between Atlanteans and us?"

The doctor laughed and waved his hand at the people walking through the streets. Allen followed his hand and then looked back at the doctor curiously, not understanding. The doctor took a few steps and placed himself next to Iris and Brad, maintaining a respectful distance from Iris. Allen shook his head, still not understanding. The doctor then walked over and pulled Amar and Bjorn together and watched Allen to see if he figured it out.

"I got it," said Bjorn excitedly. "The Atlanteans all look very similar. We do not."

"Exactly," said the doctor.

"I see that now," said Allen, looking around. "But I was wondering about things besides appearance."

"The appearance is only the hint," said the doctor as

the group of them started to make their way down the road. "The reason Atlanteans look so similar is because there is less variation in our genetics than in humans like you. Atlanteans have only twenty-two base pairs of chromosomes. You have twenty-three."

"I have one more question," said Allen, waiting until there was no one near by before asking it. "Tell me about the birth defects that have been happening."

The doctor stopped walking. He looked around very carefully.

"That is not something we discuss. I can tell simply that they are happening more frequently."

The doctor turned and shook Antonia's hand. "Thank you for allowing us to help today. I must be going."

"Wait," said Kelly.

The doctor stopped, looking around nervously.

"Is it more frequent in that end of the city?" asked Kelly, pointing off in one direction.

The doctor looked surprised at Kelly's question, then simply nodded before leaving.

Back at the apartment, Iris showed the other MacIver girls how to prepare food for the evening. Most of them were feeling more energetic than when they had returned from the pod. As they sat and ate and shared food they swapped stories about their day.

"The engine," said Kelly, blurting it out mid-conversation. "It is kind of like the one on the ship we traveled in, but ours had that living shield that fed on the radiation."

Kelly had everyone's attention now.

"We toured those engines with Helen," Kelly continued. "They have heavy sheeting protecting them. Sheeting that the Atlanteans don't know how to remove."

Kelly told them how Helen had once been a part of a team that was tasked with attempting to dismantle the protective covering over the engines, in hopes they could find a way to bypass the main controls. They never were able to remove the coverings, but one engine had cracks in its covering that they tried to make larger in hopes of using that as a way to get to the engines.

"It was that engine," Kelly said, pointing in the same direction she had shown the doctor.

"Radiation," said Antonia.

Kelly nodded.

"That could have affected Helen's baby," said Joane sadly.

"What?" asked Iris. "What baby?"

It was Allen who passed on the details of Helen's talk about the sea creature, the women and babies, and her own baby and husband.

"John got sick all of a sudden," said Iris. "He was always one of the strongest, healthiest men in Atlantis. Some speculated that because John's illness was very similar to what happened to Helen's father and grandfather, it wasn't natural. I never heard about her child."

"Wasn't natural?" asked Brad. "You mean poisoned?"

"It could have been radiation Helen carried home," speculated Antonia.

"No. I think not," said Iris. The engine project did not start until her grandfather and father were dead, because they both objected to it, no matter how Leonidis tried to justify it."

"So, John was Helen's husband?"

Iris nodded. "Is. That is not something they end simply because he is away from her."

Brad let his hand slide over to take hold of Iris' hand, trying not to draw the attention of the others. Iris took hold of his hand and covered it with the folds of her dress.

The conversation went long into the night as the MacIvers talked about the conversations they had with people isolated in the pod. They were stories that the MacIvers found not only sad but disturbing. There was a lot of fear that the city would soon be leaving, and they would be left to die.

"What if there was no pod for them to be left in?" asked Kelly. "Leonidis would be forced to let them back in the city."

"No," said Iris. "One of two things would happen. An unfortunate accident, just like the 'natural' deaths of Helen's family, or a decision of the Three, which will be decided by Leonidis' vote because he is the man and there are only two of the Three."

"Oh," said Kelly, sounding deflated.

Allen sat at the edge of the room much of the evening listening to his family talk and tell their stories. He had caught Brad holding Iris' hand, though he never let on. It made him feel sad when he saw it. When everyone seemed talked out, and the room became silent, Allen spoke up.

"I can fix the code."

This got their attention.

"I can fix it, but I will need all of you to be there with me, including you Iris," said Allen. "Because my fix will not do what I am sure Leonidis wants, which is to be the only one in control."

"Who will be in control then," asked Iris.

"There will be three," said Allen. "When there are three, we can deal with the people that have been excommunicated.   Get some sleep."

Allen wheeled his way out to the deck. He was sure he would not be sleeping that night. The others made their way to their rooms, but Sheila stopped to see Allen first. She leaned down and hugged her brother and Allen returned the hug.

"I don't know what your plan is," said Sheila. "But no matter what is, they will both be hurt."

"I saw that," said Allen.

"We all saw that," said Sheila. "Brad thinking he was being sneaky holding her hand."

Allen wanted to laugh but he could barely get a smile to his face.

"Night bro," said Sheila as she left.

"Night."

Eventually, Allen did nod off sitting in his chair on the deck. It was Iris that woke him in the morning.

"We have a guest," said Iris. "Leonidis is here."

Allen worked to re-adjust himself in his chair, feeling the stiffness of sitting in it all night.

"I told him you were out here and had asked for privacy so you could think about your computer code."

Allen nodded in thanks. At least Leonidis would not know Allen was sleeping out there. He rolled into the apartment and found Brad and Amar sitting with Leonidis.

It seemed none of his sisters were up yet. Leonidis did not waste any of his time on pleasantries.

"I need you to teach my people how to read that code."

Allen had been over this conversation in his mind, but he had hoped to have it in the presence of other Atlanteans. He was glad to hear the sound of the door opening. Leonidis was not. It was Iris' parents, and they were accompanied by Helena.

"We were coming across to confirm our daughter was being kept in the respectable way until the ceremony, which we need to discuss son," said Iris' father. "We ran into Helen on the way and invited her to bear witness, as is custom. My apologies, Leonidis. I was not aware you were here."

Leonidis' anger was apparent, but he did his best to conceal it. Allen took advantage of this interruption.

"I thought Atlanteans can not enter the control chamber unless they are part of the Three."

Helen cocked her head as she looked at Leonidis.

"Yes, that is the law," Leonidis reluctantly agreed. "But you can transfer the code elsewhere."

"It is a closed system," said Allen. "There is nowhere else to access it."

Allen let that sit for a minute.

"I am guessing that the first piece of code I was shown was entered by hand into the new system, and in the process shut your systems down."

"Is that what caused the city to shut down Leonidis?" asked Helen.

Leonidis ignored her as he stood up.

"My sons are my blood and inheritors to the position of one of the Three. By my interpretation, this means they can enter the chamber, and they will when you next access the code."

To the others in the room, this sounded like a threat, but Allen was pleased to hear it.

"After midday," said Allen, causing Leonidis to pause as he was about to leave. "If you, your sons, Helen, and my family, which includes Brad who as you said the other night is technically one of the Three, I believe I can resolve the issues."

"How," said Leonidas warily.

"You wanted Brad to stay initially. I can change some of the code to recognize the extra chromosome pair of humans."

Leonidis looked at Helen, and then Iris' parents. He was about to explode, but he was trapped by the presence of the other Atlanteans who were in the room.

"That will be suitable," said Leonidis before walking out the door.

Allen felt Brad's hand on his shoulder. "I trust you, bro."

"You should not," said Allen quietly.

It was his internal voice that found its way out. Brad did not hear it, but Amar did. Amar watched Allen carefully and saw only sadness, so he did not ask.

"I am sorry we could not intrude sooner," said Helen. "You handled that well."

"And your 'chance' arrival was perfectly timed," said Allen.

Helen laughed, and the MacIver girls entered the common area, no longer needing to pretend they were asleep in their rooms.

# Chapter 13

As they were about to enter the Aqua Nexus a young woman approached Brad. He thought he recognized her, but he wasn't sure. She shook his hand and congratulated him, then hugged Iris.

"Thank you," the girl whispered in Iris' ear, before walking off.

Iris saw the perplexed look on Brad's face.

"That was Diana, Leonidis' daughter, and the man with her is the one she is very much in love with."

"Oooooh," said Brad. "Now I recognize her."

"I used to chase after that man at one time," said Iris.

Brad's neck practically snapped as he turned to face Iris. She just giggled at the jealousy showing on Brad's face.

When they reached the top floor of the Nexus, they

found Helen waiting to greet them, along with several other men who were occupying the floor.  Allen recognized a couple of them as the men who accompanied Helen.  The rest he assumed were part of Leonidis' entourage.  Leonidis and his sons were already waiting in the control room.

"Stop," said Leonidis.  "She cannot enter."

Leonidis was pointing at Iris.  Allen started to speak but Brad interrupted him.

"There are nothing but men on this floor and for me to allow her to leave my side in this situation would be a violation of your laws," said Brad.

Allen casually rolled his chair back so he was not between Brad and Leonidis.

"The guardians assigned to Iris by her father are my sisters, and they will all be present in this room," Brad continued.  "And as your sons are linked to the Three, so is Iris through our union."

Brad held up his left hand to proudly display the bracelet he was wearing. Leonidis looked to his sons for support, but their eyes only looked to the doorways where the other men were observing the conversation from.  He looked to Helen who nodded to indicate her agreement with Brad.  Reluctantly, Leonidis backed down.

"I am sure we will have many great debates about Atlantean law in the future, Brad.

"Brad, I need you by this chair," said Allen as he rolled over to the third chair in the room that nobody had occupied in a long time. "Do not sit in it. Just watch Helen."

"Leonidis, you and your sons can watch me, and I will explain the changes I am making to the code."

This seems to settle Leonidis to a degree. Allen motioned for Helen to take her seat, and the other MacIvers spread out around the room. As the arms of Helen's chair shrouded her forearms, the screens came to life. Allen pulled out a piece of paper and handed it to one of Leonidis' sons.

"That is the code we need to change," said Allen.

He scrolled through the code on the screen until he found what he wanted.

"You see this," said Allen as he pointed up to the screen. "This string of twenty-two symbols."

From his wheelchair Allen could not reach where the characters were displayed on the screen so his pointing hand just kind of waved in the air. One of Leonidis' sons touched a spot on the screen.

"Do you mean these?" he asked.

"Yes," said Allen excitedly. You get it.

The young man looked to his father for approval which Leonidis gave him tacitly.

"Those are the DNA strings. We are going to change

that so it accepts an extra set of chromosomes.  See."

Allen quickly pointed at the paper he had handed them. As he expected, Leonidis' sons found a string of 23 symbols on the paper.

"And what is the rest of this," asked Leonidis, a note of caution still in his voice.

"That is the brilliant part," said Allen excitedly.  "Toni reminded me that Brad's children will likely carry the twenty-two chromosome pairs because of Atlanteans' stronger genetics."

"Of course," said Leonidis.

Antonia had never told Allen anything like that, but she didn't say anything.  Leonidis was taking great pride in the fact that Atlanteans had "stronger genetics."

"So," said Allen.  "The rest of the code tells the system to reset itself when the new twenty-two chromosome Atlantean is introduced into the chair.  See."

Allen randomly pointed at bits of code on the paper that Bjorn and Joane had so carefully created. He took time to explain little snippets of code and what they did, and Leonidis' sons asked many questions.  Allen answered them all, and all his answers made complete sense, for people who Allen was sure had barely a basic understanding of what the code on the screen meant.

"Are we sure that is the direction we want to go?" asked Helen.

Helen questioning the process was the trigger needed to stimulate Leonidis.

"Do it. Enter it now."

Helen was about to object until she saw Kelly's face. Kelly moved her head every so slightly in a signal not to continue.

Allen moved to the keyboard and quickly entered his code. Leonidis and his sons watched the screen, but as Allen entered and scrolled and entered and scrolled, the code he entered disappeared in the mass of symbols on the screens.

"Your station next," said Allen to Leonidis. "Your son can enter the code this time."

Leonidis' sense of caution had dissolved. In his head, he saw an opportunity. They would need Brad to get the control center completely online, but the kid in his wheelchair was making a mistake. The automatic switch of the system from human genetic code back to Atlantean meant that once Brad had started the system, he could put any Atlantean he wanted in the chair almost immediately, eliminating his need for Brad or Brad's genetic line. Leonidis didn't think Helen had noticed this flaw either. He sat down in his chair and his screens fired up.

Allen made his way to the second control panel.

"If you push this and this it will import the code from the first console."

The older son quickly pushed the two symbols and they watched the coded on the screen bounce around as it updated.  Leonidis watched with a sense of excitement. When the code stopped bouncing, Allen scrolled through it. He noticed that the console was considerably warmer than the first, which told him someone had been using it for quite a while recently.

"The third one is going to be more difficult.  It requires two people to enter symbols. One from each side of the screen so that it pulls and compares code from each of the other two panels for verification," said Allen has he made his way to where the third control panel should appear.  "The symbols have to be entered in unison."

"Just show me the symbols," said Lenonidis' second son as he volunteered.

"No," said Leonidis.  "Leave the boy to do it.  We can't afford any mistakes."

Allen noticed that he was referred to as 'the boy' but he ignored it.

"Brad, you need to sit in that chair."

Brad took a deep breath and looked around.

"Sit," said Leonidis "It is quite comfortable."

"We need to trick the chair, so Iris, you need to hold his hands as he sits back."

Brad sat back in the chair, holding onto Iris' hands, and as he did so the screen across from him flickered briefly. The flicker was long enough for Leonidis' son to push his symbols.

"Not yet!" exclaimed Allen as he spun his wheelchair around and looked at the other screens.

"Okay, good," said Allen. It didn't register.

"Pay attention, boy," said Leonidis angrily to his son.

"Okay, the second part of tricking the chair," said Allen. "Brad, you and Iris need to switch positions, but never let go of her hands."

Leonidis didn't like the sound of this. He sat upright as much as he could to watch, but Allen just turned to face the console. The screens flickered briefly again.

"Now let her hands go, Brad."

"NO!" screamed Leonidis as he attempted to jump up from his chair. The gauntlets held him tight though.

Brad let Iris' hands go and as he did, the shrouds came out of the arms of the chair and took hold of her arms. The screens flashed to life and Allen pushed two symbols, as did Leonidis' son.

"No!" screamed Leonidis again.

He struggled to free himself from the gauntlets, but as Allen had noticed the last time, that could not happen until he relaxed.  Men gathered outside the doors to the control room, waiting for direction.

"What have you done," asked Brad, as he spun Allen's wheelchair around.

"It wasn't supposed to be like that," said Allen, loud enough for the men outside the room to hear.  "It must have happened when he pushed the buttons at the wrong time."

Brad punched Allen across the jaw and would have hit him again if Joane and Amar hadn't stepped in.  Brad returned to the chair where Iris was now sitting.

"Are you okay," he asked, placing his hand gently on her face.

"I am," said Iris.

Leonidis was yelling at his sons who were trying to pull him out of his chair and causing him a lot of pain in the process.

"What is happening," asked one of the men at the door.

Allen moved to a console and scrolled the symbols on the screen. Then turned to face the crowd of men at the doors.

"You have your Three," said Allen.  "But it looks like when those buttons were pushed too early the system rebooted to some old code.  If I am reading this right, never again will the next generation of the Three be able to come from the same family as the previous generation, or any family of the existing Three."

There was a murmur rolling through the hall as Allen turned back and scrolled through the code again for dramatic effect. He turned back around and the murmur went quiet.

"There is one other thing. The Three will never be three men or three women. With each iteration, it will change from two women, as it is now, to two men, to two women, and continue that cycle."

Allen heard Leonidis finally get out of his chair. He turned to see him shove his sons away from him, his arms bloodied from his struggle.

"You did this," Leonidis yelled as he quickly approached Allen. "You did this."

"I am sorry," said Allen. "I should have been more clear about when your son should push those symbols. Perhaps it was a language barrier."

Leonidis moved as though he was going to strike Allen, but he saw the men watching from the door. He collected himself and tried to sound calm.

"We have the Three," he said, and then quickly found his way out of the control chamber with his sons following close behind.

Helen had got up from her chair as well. She looked at Allen and bowed silently, placing her hand over her heart, before walking over to where Iris was seated.

"Take a deep breath and just think about those gauntlets coming off, Iris."

Iris followed Helen's direction and the gauntlets released. Brad quickly pulled her up from the chair and hugged her.

"I am sorry," he said. "I didn't know."

"I know," said Iris. "At least we are keeping it in the family."

Brad tipped his head back so he could see Iris' face. She had a smile. He smiled back at her.

"You need to come with me, Iris," said Helen quietly. "We need to make sure the city knows before a different story is circulated."

Iris understood and she followed Helen, Brad close behind.

"You did this," said Brad angrily as they walked by Allen. "I won't forget this."

"Go." Allen directed the other MacIvers. "Stay with them. Don't leave them alone."

The other MacIvers followed Brad and Iris, except for Sheila, and when everyone was gone, Sheila sat on the floor and rested her head on Allen's knees.

"You can cry now," she said softly, and Allen did.

# Chapter 14

When Sheila and Allen returned to the apartment everyone else was already there. They found four men standing outside the apartment door, but the quickly moved aside, clearing the way for Allen and Sheila to go in. All of the MacIvers were sitting in the common area, as were Iris' parents and Helen.

"Can we talk, Brad?"

"If you have anything to say, you can say it to all of us," said Brad angrily.

Iris put a gentle hand on Brad, but he pushed it away.

"He needs to explain it to all of us."

"It wasn't an accident," said Allen. "I knew exactly what I was doing, and I saw no other way to do it."

Brad started to get up, but Iris held him down.

"We have seen and read about leaders like Leonidis. Every move he has made has been to place all the power in his family. He even kills people for it."

Helen nodded as Allen spoke.

"He wants a society of perfect people, so he kills people like me. He wants a society where men rule over women. The Atlanteans needed the Three. All Three. "

Allen paused as he sorted through his thoughts.

"Changing the program was the easy part, but choosing who that third person was going to be was not. It could never have been you, Brad. It had to be an Atlantean. I could not change that in the code."

"Back home, we would have had a vote or election of some kind, but we did not have time for that. I had to choose someone I trust, and you trust Iris, so I trust Iris Brad."

Allen paused again.

"When it came down to it, Iris was the only Atlantean woman I trusted that I could get in that control room."

"Why did it have to be a woman?" asked Bjorn.

"Because some things need to change quickly in this culture," said Kelly.

Allen nodded.

"You knew what you were going to do," said Brad. "Why didn't you tell us?

"I didn't tell you because…because you would have said no. You care for her more than I think even you know. I didn't tell the others because they care for you and wouldn't want to see you hurt. I chose to carry that burden alone."

"So, you chose to hurt Iris and me," said Brad angrily.

"Yes," said Allen as he hung his head.

The room was quiet. The silence was heavy on Allen and he started to make his way to his room.

"Please wait," said Iris.

Iris walked up to Allen and took his hand in hers.

"You chose what would protect me and make me happy. As one of the Three, I am safe from everything and I don't need to leave my family and friends and home. Brad would have made the same choice for me. Thank you for not forcing him to choose."

Iris gave Allen a gentle kiss on the cheek. Allen nodded and made his way to his room.

"It is up to you guys to save the people in the pod," he said.

Allen wished there was a door in his room he could shut.  Instead, he lowered himself to the sleeping pad a pulled the blanket over his head.

# Chapter 15

"Let's figure this out," said Brad.

Iris sat back down beside him, and took his hand in hers, not making any attempt to hide it.

"We can kill two birds with one stone," said Kelly.

Helen looked very confused at that statement. Kelly realized that she had not seen any birds or animals of any kind since they had arrived on Europa, except the marine creatures outside the dome, and the ones that were in the market for food.

"Two fish with one spear?" said Kelly, questioning her simile.

Helen nodded her understanding.

Helen wasn't present for the conversation the MacIvers had about the birth defects, and it was important she understood the reasoning behind what Kelly was about to propose.  Kelly didn't know how to explain it though without bringing up traumatic memories for Helen.  Sheila noticed Kelly struggling for the right words and jumped in.

"Perhaps I can start this, and Toni can help me out with the medical portion," offered Sheila.

Kelly looked relieved as Sheila tried to sum up the conversation they had the previous night.  Sheila included the details of the drive of the ship they arrived on and Kelly's theory that the engines of the Atlantis were similar.  Helen was astounded at the concept of living shielding.  It was when Antonia entered the conversation and began to describe how radiation could affect living objects that Helen instinctively placed her hand over her abdomen.

"It was my fault," said Helen.

"No said Sheila.  You did not know."

"The thing is Helen, that radiation contamination can travel on bodies and clothing, and even in the air," said Kelly.  "It all makes sense when you consider that most of the …illnesses that come from radiation exposure are in the corner of the city."

Helen stood up and paced.

"How do you know that?"

"One of the doctors," said Sheila.

Helen continued pacing.

"We did succeed at making the cracks slightly larger, but we could not close them up afterward. And the entirety of my team did not end their lives well. Aside from John and I, they are all gone."

"That is where you met John?" asked Sheila.

Helen stopped pacing and a little smile replaced her stressed look as she remembered.

"It is," she said softly."

"I think I have a fix, but I don't know how to test it," said Kelly.

Kelly explained that by using the same material the dome was made out of, they could fabricate a containment area. She knew that they could not create enough of the dome material in the time they had, but they could repurpose the dome off one of the pods. Because three of the pods contained food and supplies that would need to keep harvesting until the last minute, the only option would be to move the people out of the fourth pod and use that dome.

"That is quite brilliant," said Iris' mother.

"Except we don't know how to test to see if it will work," said Kelly.

"Rocks."

Heads turned towards Deane.

"Glow in the dark rocks," said Deane. "Some react to radiation. There has to be some on the ocean floor. If we get some and put them in a box of your dome material, put it near the leak, in the dark, we will know if the dome material keeps it out."

"Students make small boxes with the material as part of their training, so that is easy to get," said Helen.

"I can walk the floor and search for rocks," said Iris' mother.

"The ocean floor?"

"Is there another, Amar?" asked Iris' mother jokingly.

"She does it every day," said Iris. "It is her designated task."

"Cool," Amar said nodding.

"Let's get moving then," said Brad.

"We need to involve Leonidis," said Iris.

"Why?" asked Amar.

"Leonidis is unpredictable. If he thinks we are doing things behind his back he will act in fear. If we involve him, it will look better to him, and better for him to the people," explained Iris.

"You are right," said Helen. "I will send a messenger and ask him to meet us."

"Keep your friends close, and your enemies closer," said Brad.

"What is that," asked Iris' father.

"Just a saying from home."

"I will have to remember that," said Iris' Father.

Helen stopped Iris as the family left the apartment. She suggested she ask one of her assistants to remain behind and see that no one entered the apartment, since Allen was in there alone. Iris did that after double-checking with Brad about asking Allen to join them, which Brad was having none of.

The third station was the name of the area the MacIvers were entering. Each of the engine modules had been given a number and it was number three that had the cracked shielding. After getting some suggestions from Deane, Iris' mother decided to take on of the small dome material boxes out to the floor with her. When Leonidis arrived she was already out walking the ocean floor.

"What is going on here?" asked Leonidis.

"We are testing a theory," said Kelly. "Iris and Helen thought you should be part of this.

Leonidis noticed that many people were watching, and he nodded to acknowledge Helen and Iris' presence.

"We believe that radioactive poison is leaking from the cracked shielding on that engine and that we can find reactive rocks on the ocean floor that will show us when we are safe."

"Those engines have not run in thousands of years," said Leonidis. "We don't even know if they will run now."

"The technology holds vast amounts of energy in reserve if it is like our ship."

"Is this another one of your boy's ideas?"

Leonidis looked around and didn't see Allen. He quickly whispered something to the man behind him who left them.

"Do you mean Allen?" asked Iris. She continued without waiting for an answer. "No. It was Kelly's theory and Deane's solution."

Leonidis nodded and turned to watch Iris' mother out on the ocean floor. As she would near something glowing she would kick at it gently. If it moved away, it was alive and not what they were looking for. If it didn't move she would pick it up and put it in the box she was holding and close the box. If it didn't stop glowing she dumped it out and moved to the next one that caught her eye.

Iris' mother had picked up a few dozen rocks and was about to give up when she noticed a larger rock that glowed a slightly different color from the rest. She picked it up and dropped it in the box. The moment she closed the lid the glow slowly dimmed down to nothing. She opened the box and the rock glowed again until she closed it. She excitedly bounced across the ocean floor in big steps towards the main dome. When she could make out the faces of the people inside, she opened the box and a glow filled the water in front of her. She closed the box and the glow disappeared.

Kelly pumped her fist in the air. "Yes!!" Then she gave Deane a bear hug.

"I take it that is a good sign," said Leonidis.

"When Kelly is that happy, it is always a good sign because it rarely happens," said Bjorn who was standing next to Leonidis.

Leonidis actually managed a laugh.

Kelly eagerly took the box from Iris' mother when she returned.

"Thank you. You should go home now," said Kelly.

"And spend some time in a hot shower," suggested Antonia.

Iris' parents left and made their way home. They didn't notice that Iris' assistant was no longer standing outside the door to the MacIvers.

Kelly led everyone else, including Leonidis to the engine chamber. She left the box open as they walked and as they got closer to the engine the brighter the rock glowed. Kelly saw no reason to go any closer when the rock became so bright you couldn't make out its outline anymore. She turned and faced the people behind her. It was more than just her family and Helen. Other Atlanteans that had been observing them had also followed them.

"Close it, Leonidis."

Leonidis noticed the people just as Kelly had, so he made a show of closing the box. As soon as it did the glow began to fade, and quickly it became just a dull grey rock in a clear box.

"You have found a way to protect them," said Kelly, loud enough for people in the crowed to hear.

Leonidis could hear the chatter staring in the crowd of Atlanteans. He was trapped in Kelly's little charade, but it made him out to be the leader and perhaps hero, so he wasn't going to fight the process.

"What do you suggest we do next," he asked the MacIvers.

It was Helen who answered.

"We need to find enough dome material to seal the area. We should take the night to think on it and meet as the Three in the morning."

The crowd was liking what they were hearing, and Leonidis was skilled at reading groups of people.

"I agree. Outside the marketplace. It would be good for everyone to observe how the Three work together."

Leonidis saw this as an opportunity. He would have the support of all the men, and he was confident that after they returned to the MacIver apartment, Helen and Iris would follow his lead in the morning.

"You should all return home," said Helen. "Be safe"

The Atlanteans quickly cleared out of the area, and the MacIvers were not far behind. Helen stayed with the MacIvers, wanting to plan and prepare with Iris for the morning. There was something odd about Leonidis embracing the idea of a public meeting. As they approached the apartment it was one of Helen's assistants that stopped them. He pointed out that there was no man at the door.

Without thinking Brad raced into the apartment where he came face to chest with John. John held a finger up to his mouth making the sign for Brad to be quiet.

"Your brother is sleeping," said John quietly.

Brad backed away from John and down the hall to Allen's door, never taking his eyes off John. He turned his head long enough to see that Allen was on the floor, still breathing, asleep.

Not hearing anything from inside the apartment the rest of the MacIvers entered to investigate. They all stopped at the sight of John, except for Helen who ran forward and jumped into John's open arms. They held a long embrace followed by a passionate kiss.

"Where is the man we left to watch the door?" asked Brad.

"I suggested he go home to his family," said John. "He didn't even argue. Just left."

Brad laughed, completely understanding the thoughts the man had when John approached him.

"But why are you here?" asked Helen. "You are not supposed to be in the city unless invited."

"I was invited," said John in a serious tone. "By one of Leonidis men. With a promise I would not have to leave if I silenced the boy in the wheelchair."

Everyone looked at Brad.

"He is sleeping," said Brad.

"I silenced him," said John. "I talked his ear off until he couldn't stay awake any longer. Silence."

Helen hugged John again as he laughed his jolly laugh.

"You should be worried about me," said John. "That boy can talk. I almost fell asleep first."

"I hear you," said Allen.

Sheila approached John and shook his hand. She could tell he had something to say but wasn't sure how to bring it up.

"What did you and my talkative brother talk about?" asked Sheila.

"The personal sacrifices we have to make for those we

love sometimes. It was a subject we both could relate to."

Helen couldn't help herself. She gave John another hug, her arms barely going half the way around him. John looked over her head at Brad who just turned away and walked outside to the deck.

"Anyway, I thought I would see about hanging around a while. I understand that our newest member of the Three may be looking for a new assistant."

John gently unwrapped Helen's arms from his waist and made his way over to Iris, where he bowed deeply.

"The choice of you as one of the Three is one the people I know approve of."

"Stand up. I am not royalty."

John stood tall. Iris looked at Helen who nodded.

"It would seem I no longer have that position open, John."

John nodded his head sadly.

"I understand. I will return to the pod."

Helen spoke some harsh words in Atlantean and John laughed loudly.

"Oh. You meant I just filled the position. Thank you!"

John picked Iris right up off the floor with his hug. He set her down gently when he realized what he had done.

# Chapter 16

There was a big crowd gathered at the market when the MacIvers arrived. They were cheerfully greeted, as were Iris and John. Iris and Helen each took a seat at the triangular table and John assumed his position standing just behind Iris. Leonidis arrived fashionably late, as he tended to do, making a commotion as he worked his way through the crowd and stopped to talk to everyone. His demeanor quickly changed when he got to the front of the crowd and saw John standing behind Iris.

"One of my assistants had to deal with family obligations, so I recruited John," said Iris calmly. It was easy to hide her nervousness in her voice when she had John towering behind her. "Helen also approved of this choice. It was a good one, don't you think?

Iris had turned to the crowd when she asked the question and the crowed cheered.

Leonidis took his seat at the table, noticing Allen as he did so. He quickly realized that any advantage he thought he had no longer existed. He called for the room to be quiet. He told the crowd about the discovery that radiation was poisoning Atlanteans, but that he had now found a way to contain it, using Kelly's own words to take credit.

"If Helen and John had not opened that crack many years ago we would not be in this position," said Leonidis. "Now we have to find a way to fix it, or risk more lives as we take flight, and unfortunately there is no way for us to produce enough dome material in such a short time."

Leonidis watched and waited for the crowd to turn on Helen and John, but it did not happen.

"We are grateful for your discovery of the dome materials ability," said Iris, navigating this meeting as though she had been doing it for years. "Our guests suggested that if we sacrifice one of the outer pods, we could recover enough material to shield the engine."

Leonidis looked at Iris with a cold stare. Iris maintained her gentle smile, but John's face returned the cold stare, causing Leonidis to turn away.

"We have to harvest every last bit of food from three of those domes. We would only be putting ourselves at risk if we did not," said Helen. "But we can bring home the people in the fourth dome, bring them back to the city, and dismantle that dome immediately."

"Or we could not bring them back, and reduce the load on our resources," said Leonidis coldly. "There will only be limited supplies until we resettle."

A murmur went through the crowd. Leonidis liked the sound of that.

"Bring them back," John said, his deep voice booming through the crowd.

Leonidis stood up and slammed his fist on the table.

"You are an assistant, and not entitled to speak as one of the Three."

"He is my assistant," said Iris. "And entitled to be heard as a citizen, just as we are required by the laws to listen to the citizens."

Leonidis signaled for his assistants to come forward. They did not move. John's head was barely moving from side to side, but they got the message that they should not move.

"Bring them back," a voice from the crowd called out.

A second voice followed, and the crowd joined in and made it a chant.

"Bring them back. Bring them back. Bring them back."

Helen held up her hand to quiet the crowd, but it went unnoticed. Helen's assistants held up their hands but theirs went unnoticed as well. John raised his hand and the crowd quickly went silent. Leonidis was sitting back down, but he was so angry he was vibrating.

"I say we bring them back and re-purpose their pod," said Helen.

"I agree," said Iris.

"I do not," said Leonidis, staring intently at Helen, challenging her.

"Having made the first vote, I declare that the Three have spoken and we will bring them back."

The crowd cheered and Leonidis stormed away. His assistants did not follow him. Brad stepped in front of the crowd.

"We are looking for knowledgeable and strong men, and women, to volunteer for this work. Please come up and see me if you wish to help."

Brad turned and helped Iris up from her chair. She was shaking so Brad wrapped his hand around her arm to steady her.

You did a better job than I ever could have, my love."

Brad stopped, catching himself as he heard his own words. He turned to see Iris looking into his eyes.

"Only because I had the support of you, and your family, and John," said Iris. "My love."

Brad blushed, but he felt as big as John looked. He walked Iris back to his sisters, John staying close behind.

"She is your responsibility while I work," said Brad.

His sisters pulled Iris in, and a big group hug followed. Brad returned to the front to help Helen put their plan to work. He has to push his way through the crowd to get to the front.

"Have we got any volunteers?" Brad asked Helen as he sat down beside her.

Helen waved her hand at the crowd in front of the table.

"All of them?" said Brad. It looked as though nobody had left.

"All of them," said Helen.

Helen had already sent people to bring back everybody from the dome and the doctors were gathering equipment and medication so they could treat each one of them as they re-entered the city. There were three other men also sitting at the table whom Helen introduced as the chief architect, chief builder, and chief of transportation. A woman sat at the table also who Helen did not recognize.

"You asked for women. You need a woman to lead the women," she said boldly.

Helen smiled and nodded.  That was good enough for Brad.  Word went out to the crowd that they would be called as they were needed. The crowd quickly thinned out, though many just chose to sit and wait in the square for an assignment.  By the time the last of the people from the pod had been brought to the city, they had a detailed plan in place.  A set of gates closed as the last person came through the tunnel and all valves and vents were opened.  The ocean rushed in to fill the pod and as it did a crew worked to weld all the valves and ports permanently closed.

People gathered along the edge of the dome and watched as the pod filled with water.  An air pocket formed at the peak of its dome and Brad though that may have missed opening a vent.  He was concerned, but Helen did not seem to be, so Brad waited and watched with the others.  He heard the unmistakable sound of metal under stress and then the main dome shook as the dome on the pod separated from its floor.

"Is that what we wanted to happen?" asked Brad.

"Exactly," said the chief architect.

Viewing spaces opened up as many people walked away and made their way to the Aqua Nexus.  Brad watched and waited when he said floor walkers moving towards the pod. A lot of them.  The walkers surrounded the pod, extended the rods they were carrying, and somehow attached the rods to the sides of the now loose dome.  Working in unison they lifted the dome and started walking it away from its foundation.

"The domes are basically held in place by the weight of the water over them," said Kelly as she took a spot beside Brad. "When they let in all that water it equalized the pressure inside and out of the dome. That air bubble at the top created just enough pressure to lift is away from the foundation."

Brad looked at his sister with admiration.

"You have been reading books in secret, haven't you? Secretly surfing engineering websites in the middle of the night."

Kelly laughed.

"Just have a knack for it, I guess. Like Toni and her doctor stuff."

"How are they lifting it though?" asked Brad.

Kelly explained how the air bubble created just enough upward pressure that the dome was suspended in the water. The walkers were just pushing it along and making sure it didn't flip. Brad had understood the plan was to carry the dome material to the other side of the dome by going around rather than through the city. He had just assumed it would be in pieces.

"Let's get you to the other side," said Kelly "Then we will put your skills to work."

Brad was excited. He would be working with the builders to assemble the material as a protective shield. This was going to place him directly in front of the crack though, exposing him to a lot of radiation.  Without proper radiation suits, it was a risk, but the workers were going to use the same dive suits the walkers used, and they would only be allowed to work a short time in that area.  They took their time as they walked through the city.  It would be a while before the walkers reached the other side with the separated dome.

The atmosphere was different in the city.  Since arriving Brad had felt like he was at some formal dinner, with everyone dressed in their best outfits and going out of their way to be nice.  Today it felt much more relaxed, despite the doom they were facing.  He mentioned this to his sister and she looked at him curiously.

"What if I suggested that maybe it isn't a change in the city, but a change in you, like you belong here."

Brad shrugged his shoulders.

"Anything is possible, I guess.  Just seems different," said Brad.

"She is an amazing young woman, isn't she?" said Kelly.

"Yes, she is," said Brad as he touched his bracelet.

It took a few steps for Brad to realize what Kelly was hinting at.  He gave her a dirty look and held her hands up.

"I won't dig anymore."

Brad wanted to be mad at Kelly, but he didn't have it in him, and he knew why she was digging. Besides, all his anger was saved for Allen.

A MacIver Kids Adveture by Lawrence Nault

# Chapter 17

The walkers came in, tired and exhausted. They passed by a second group of people suited up in different dive suits going out as they came in. The second group wore heavier suits with a variety of tools clipped to their belts. For every walker that came in, there was someone there to help them out of their suit and give them food and water.

As soon as the last walker was back on the main level a mass of Atlanteans filled the stair wells and halls. This was the only way to move the pieces of the dome up several levels and down to the engine chamber. The elevators would not be able to handle the loads. The second group of divers cut into the small dome that had now been upended and the air pocket released. As the first piece made its way into the city a workers began a chant as they passed it up the stairs and to the engine chamber.

The chant reverberated throughout the city, the dome acting as an amphitheater. People stopped what they were doing to listen.

"Do you know what a choir of angels is," Bjorn as one of the Atlanteans near him.

"Yes, I do," said the man. "And you are right."

Leonidis was not enjoying the chanting. It irritated him and reminded him of his failure and public humiliation that morning. He stood in his office cursing, his daughter standing in the middle of the room with her head bowed. Leonidis picked up a vial off the desk in front of him.

"Is this it?"

"Yes, Sir," replied Diana.

"Is there enough there?"

Leonidis held up the vial and shook it. It contained skin tissue and hairs that Diana had scraped off of Brad when she shook his hand.

"The doctor says there is," said Diana.

Leonidis set it down gently on his desk, glancing at the two other vials that were there also.

"And these are,"

"From your son's, Sir," replied Diana, struggling to hold back her tears.

"Excellent," said Leonidis, his smile verging on evil. "Have them call the doctor. We will do it here so I can watch and make sure it happens."

Deana broke down in tears and her father smacked her with the back of his hand.

"Your husband will never know he was not the father. This is for your family. You should be proud to make this sacrifice."

"Yes, Sir," said Diana as she returned to her position standing in the center of the room.

Across the city the work on the shield progressed smoothly, but slowly. The day turned into evening and evening into night. Workers switched each other off in shifts. Helen was present in the early hours of the morning when the last piece of the dome material went into place and the glow on the rock dimmed. She wanted to cheer but she was too exhausted.

"You have done it," said Helen, as she found a place to sit on the floor. "Tell everyone they have done it and to go home and get some sleep."

The workers who were in the chamber lifted their masks off and hugged each other. The hugs passed down the line as the message that they had succeeded was passed along. Slowly the stairways and halls cleared and divers returned from outside. The last man gathered his tools before leaving the engine chamber.

"We all know that you and your husband did not cause those cracks. Thank you for working for us and with us."

Helen watched as the man walked away. She remained sitting there, staring at the cracks, her hand resting on her abdomen. Did Leonidis know when he sent her and John in there? Did he really kill her father and grandfather? And their child. The one they had waited so long for. She remembered grateful it had been born dead because it was so malformed, but was that her fault of Leonidis'? Helen was finding it hard not to hate. She fell asleep in the chamber. It was Brad and Kelly that woke Helen up. Kelly held the rock in her hand.

"It looks like you did it," said Kelly.

"No, we did it. You, me, your brothers and sisters, and the entire city. "

"Come get breakfast," said Brad. "You must be hungry."

As they approached the market square cheers sounded. There was a celebration going on.

"We need to avoid that," said Helen.

"Agreed," said Brad.

They wove their way through the streets and avoided the party, making their way back to the MacIver apartment. John greeted his wife with a hug and kiss, then sent her off to a room telling her to get some real sleep. Helen didn't argue with him.

Iris greeted Brad in much the same way, with a hug and a gentle kiss on the lips. Bjorn's jaw dropped and Joane told him to close his mouth a grow up. Brad said nothing. He did not expect that his first kiss would be in front of his family that morning.

"Is that not how you do it?" asked Iris innocently, trying to read the strange look on Brad's face. "I asked your sisters, and they said that is how I should welcome you home."

"That was perfect," said Brad.

"Good. Now come eat," said Iris as she grabbed Brad's hand and led him to the deck where she had warm tea and a tray of food waiting for him.

"You are spoiling him," said Antonia as she stuck her head outside for a brief moment.

"Of course. I only have a little time left to do that."

Antonia saw the look on Brad's face and quickly returned inside. Iris saw the look too.

"I know you have to go home with your family."

"You are my family," said Brad. "And if Allen didn't pull his little stunt we would not be having this conversation."

Brad played with the bracelet on his wrist, then took hold of Iris' hand and touched her bracelet.

"This started by accident. I know that. And it has only been a short time. But you have to know that I would do it again because we belong together. I cannot leave you alone and this bracelet means if I leave you will be alone, forever, and so will I.

"I don't believe in accidents, my love," said Iris. "I believe in fate, and fate brought you across the universe to me."

Iris wiped a tear from the corner of her eye.

"I am committed to this union as much as you are, and not because I have to or because of my culture. It is because I want to. In your culture, you may still be seen as a boy, but here, by my people and by me, you are a great man, with a heart bigger than John's."

Brad opened his arms and Iris cuddled up to his chest. He could feel her tears soaking through his shirt.

"When I call you my love, Brad, it is not because that is what you call me. It is because that is what you are. I do love you."

"I love you too, Iris," said Brad, then he kissed her gently on her head.

When her tears had stopped Iris stood up. She reached her left hand out and gently touched her bracelet to Brad's. They rang like a tuning fork and Brad could feel the vibrations through his body.

"That is the final step of the ceremony. The vibrations that announce to the universe that I am yours, and you are mine, forever and into the next life."

"Forever and into the next life," said Brad.

"I will get you a warm tea now."

Iris returned into the apartment to get the tea. Brad could see his family watching him from inside. He got up and walked past them and down the hall, passing Allen's room on the way. He noticed Allen was sitting in his room and he stopped, then backed up a step.

"You did this," Brad said, just loud enough for Allen to hear him, and then he continued on to his room.

Allen didn't move or say anything. He knew Brad was right.

Iris' parents come over later in the morning, letting themselves in as was the Atlantean custom. Brad made is way over to greet them, shaking her father's hand. Her mother grabbed Brad's left hand and lifted it, showing her husband.

"Forever and into the next life?"

Brad nodded. "Forever and into the next life, sir"

Iris' father pulled Brad in and hugged him with one arm while shaking his hand with the other.

"I will proudly call you son forever and into the next life, wherever you are."

"You should know, those bracelets only change to that color when there is a true, emotional bond."

Brad looked at his bracelet as Iris' father loosened his hold.  He never noticed that it had changed colors.  He barely got a look at it before her mother pulled him in for a hug.

"Forever and into the next life," she said as she hugged him.

"Forever and into the next life," said Brad.

The MacIvers watched the interactions with curiosity, not quite sure what was going on.  Helen pushed herself up against John, remembering their union ceremony.

As soon as Iris' mother let Brad go she ran over to her daughter, and they hugged and bounced around.

Amar looked at Brad, holding his hands in the air near his shoulders, palms up.

"Atlantean stuff," said Brad.  "You wouldn't understand."

Iris approached her father, watching his face.

"Do you approve?"

"Of course I approve," he said as he wrapped his arms around his daughter.  "There could be no better choice.  Did you see this?

Her father lifted her left hand so they could both see her bracelet.

"Wasn't that gold," asked Bjorn.

The once gold bracelet was an iridescent metallic rainbow.

"I did," Iris said to her father.

"I hate to interrupt," said Helen. "But Leonidis has summoned us for a test start of the engines. You are explicitly not invited, Allen. Kelly is directly invited and of course, Brad will be expected, though not allowed in the control room this time as Iris is your superior."

"Nice!!" said Joane. "You go, girl!"

Allen returned to his room. For the first time in his life he was feeling isolated from his family. Being told he was specifically not invited to something only triggered those feelings of isolation more. He instinctively reached down to pet Fritter, but his hand only found air. He could understand why Brad felt the way he did, and knowing Brad, Allen wasn't sure the two of them would recover. He wasn't sure why all his sisters seemed to have a hate on for him and even Amar seemed to want to keep his distance. Only Bjorn seemed unphased by it all.

"We are all going for a walkabout around town," said Antonia who was standing in his doorway. "Let's go."

"You go ahead," said Allen. "I am fine here."

"If you stay home, the others have to stay as well to make sure you are safe," said Antonia in an exasperated tone. "We all want to go, so let's go."

# Chapter 18

The MacIvers wandered through the streets and pathways of Atlantis. Without any destination in mind, or concern for having to get something done weighing on them the view was different. They took the time to admire the architecture and artwork that was everywhere. They stopped to talk to people, and people stopped to talk to them. The city had quickly returned to its usual activities, almost as though the previous day hadn't happened. Several times throughout their walk they found themselves calling back for Bjorn to catch up after realizing he was busy making yet another sketch and had not seen them walk away.

A young child approached the MacIvers, her mother standing back and watching. Sheila recognized the mother and her daughter from the pod. The child didn't say anything, but she tied a fabric bracelet around the wrist of each of the MacIver girls. The MacIvers gushed over the bracelets and Sheila took a moment to talk to the mother.

"She is so happy to see you," said the mother. "She worked so hard making those bracelets after you came to see us in that other place. I didn't have the heart to tell her we would probably never see you again. And yet, here we are."

"I am happy we came this way," said Sheila. "Have they found a place for you to live in the city?

The woman pointed to the building behind her.

"There was always room for us," said the woman. "Some people, somebody, just didn't want to have us in the city."

The woman was looking past Sheila as she talked, watching her daughter interact with the MacIvers.

"What is that your sister is doing?"

Sheila turned so she could see what was going on.

"Can your daughter hear?" asked Sheila.

"No," said the woman nervously.

Sheila put her hand on the woman's arm to calm her. She guessed that was why they had been sent to the pod.

"Jo has a friend like your daughter where we come from. Her friend uses sign language and Jo has learned some of it from her. It looks like Jo is showing your daughter some of that sign language."

The mother watched her daughter. She had not seen so much joy on her face in a long time, and at times it seemed like she was having a real conversation with Joane. Joane noticed the girl's mother watching intently, so she took the girl by her hand and brought her to her mother. When Joane let go of her hand, the girl looked up nervously at her. Joane just smiled.

Looking at her mother, the girl pointed to her own eye, then crossed her wrists over her chest, then pointed at her mother. The mother looked confused.

"It is in my language," said Joane, "so it might not translate well."

Joane looked at the little girl and encouraged her to do it one more time.

"I," said Joane as the girl pointed at her eye.

"Love," said Joane as the girl crossed her wrists over her chest.

The moment the little girl pointed the mother dropped to her knees, sobbing as she hugged her daughter.

"Guess I didn't need to translate that last one," Joane whispered to Sheila.

The mother pushed her daughter back and then made the same signs herself. The little girl jumped up and wrapped her arms around her mother's neck.

"We have nothing like this. There has not been anyone else like her so we thought she wouldn't be able or capable of really communicating," the woman said as she stood up with her daughter in her arms. "Can you teach me?"

Joane explained that they would not be there long enough, but it didn't matter. Since she was the first, they could make their own hand signs for everything. Their own secret language that her daughter could share with friends and others.

"We can do that," the woman said. "I don't know why I didn't think of it myself."

"Because we fear what we don't understand, instead of trying to understand what we fear," said Allen, who had moved himself closer.

The woman looked at Allen.

"Did they do that to you?" she asked.

"Some still do," but I am not the first where I come from.

"Can you ask her why she does this," said the mother, turning back to Joane and moving pointing to her daughter's hand on her throat.

Joane smiled a big smile. The little girl smiled back just as big.

"Hum a note," said Joane.

The woman only looked back at her. Joane hummed a note, then Sheila joined in. The woman, understanding now, hummed a note as well. As they hummed Joane moved the little girl's hand from her mother's throat to Sheila's, to her own, and then put the girl's hand on her own throat. She let go of the girl's hand and watched.

The little girl moved her hand back to her mother's throat and held it there for a moment, then she put her hand back on her own throat. Joane encouraged the girl with her eyes. Then she heard it. A small quiet hum that got loud quickly. The mother jumped, almost dropping her daughter.

"I didn't know. I didn't know. I have to show this to her father."

They watched her run into the building with her daughter in her arms. Joane and Sheila high-fived each other. Then the MacIvers continued on their exploration of the city. They soon found themselves walking past the campus where Iris' father worked.

"I am going to go in here, said Bjorn.

The ground under their feet vibrated and everyone and everything stopped moving for a moment.

"Must be the engines," said Antonia, as everyone started moving around them again.

"I will be a while," said Bjorn. "I will come home with Iris' father. You guys keep going."

"Someone should stay with you," said Antonia.

"I will be fine," said Bjorn.

"I will stay," said Allen. He had felt like the only reason he was invited on this walk was so nobody had to stay home with him, so this provided an opportunity for him to separate himself from the others.

"That's a good idea," said Joane. "Amar is with us so we will be good."

Sheila could see in Allen's eyes that Joane's comment hurt him. She knew Joane meant nothing mean by it, but she also knew that Allen was hurting and sensitive to everything at the moment. There was nothing she could do or say that would help at the moment.

"I have something I want to do as a surprise for Brad and Iris," said Bjorn as they made the way through the halls of the campus. "I am just going to be in the back of one of the classes that Iris' father is teaching. There is like a library across the hall if you want something to do while you wait."

Allen liked that idea. Bjorn walked with him into the library and even introduced Allen to a couple of students who were there before going on his way. When Iris' father saw Bjorn at the door he pointed to the back of the room. Bjorn made his way to the back while the class continued.

The MacIvers sat at a table in the market square, having something to eat and drink. There were many Atlanteans around them. Some would stop and talk to them for a few moments. Others would just say hello as they walked by. The city began to shake again, more violently than the first time. This time the people around them found something to hold on to as one side of the city lifted higher than the other, then fell quickly.

"I don't think that is how it is supposed to work," said Allen.

Sheila didn't even have to look around to feel the tension in the Atlanteans in the square.

———————————

"One of you is not following my directions," screamed Leonidis. "We don't have time for stubborn women!"

Brad walked around the room, looking at the screens. Leonidis' sons were also there. Everyone else remained outside the control room.

"This looks like a video game I play," said Brad.

"What does a child's game have to do with any of this?" Leonidis asked angrily.

"Just hear him out please," said Iris kindly.

"Look," said Brad, pointing at one of the screens. "There are four bars here, but they remain the same color all the time. Under those bars is this other horizontal one that has this line through the middle. I watched. When you guys fired the engines this horizontal bar changed color at the bottom."

Leonidis looked at his sons, and both said they saw the same change.

"You are all trying to control all the engines at once, right? But there are four engines and three control stations. What if each of these vertical bars is an engine" said Brad as he touched the screen.

As soon as Brad's hand touched the screen, Leonidis' oldest son grabbed his arm.

"Sorry," said Brad. He had been warned earlier not to touch any of the panels. "I got a little carried away."

"Continue," said Leonidis.

Brad looked at Leonidis' son with a look that let him know he was only holding his arm because Brad was allowing it. Leonidis' son quickly released his grip.

"Okay. And what if this horizontal bar is overall power? Try something. One of you. Just one of you, try to power the engines."

"I will," said Leonidis.

Leonidis sat back in his chair and thought about powering the engines. A small portion of the horizontal bar changed color. Leonidis saw the change and thought about more power, and more of the bar changed color. Leonidis felt a challenge now to see how much power he could get and as he did so, the city began to vibrate.

"Whoa. Whoa," said Brad.

Leonidis let up and the city stopped vibrating.

"If this is the power," said Brad. "And you fire it up all the way without using it…Boom."

The Atlanteans didn't understand the word, but the motion Brad made with his hands told them exactly what he meant.

"Now you try it, Helen. Just to here," said Brad touching the screen again.

Leonidis' son moved to grab Brad again, but Leonidis stopped him. Helen thought about powering up the engines. Nothing happened. She was about to give up when the color started changing. She got excited and immediately the color moved past the position where Brad was holding his finger, but she quickly let up and it returned down to zero.

"Your turn," Leonidis said to Iris.

Immediately the bar lit up and the color changed right up to where Brad was holding his finger. She held it here for a second and then let it go. Brad looked at Leonidis, waiting for permission to continue. Leonidis nodded.

"We have power," said Brad excitedly, but we need to send that power somewhere. Iris, you had the best control of the power so fire up the engines, just a bit. We don't want to tip the city again. Leonidis, you try to light up these four vertical bars."

Iris brought up the power of the engines. Leonidis tried to light up the four vertical bars, but he could only manage two at a time.  It switched from the two on the left to the two on the right and bounced back and forth. As the color bounced between the left and right bars the ship began to wobble from side to side.  Helen said something in Atlantean and there was color in all four bars and the city stopped wobbling.  A gentle thrum filled the air.

Leonidis called out and Brad felt the city tilt to his left. He called out again and the city tilted to the right. Then they tilted it back and forth.  Iris said something in her language and Brad the city followed a tilt around its circumference like a coin spinning down on a tabletop.

"Are we having fun," Brad asked, knowing the answer from the smile on everybody's face.

"More power," said Leonidis excitedly.

"No," Helen shouted, and Iris immediately powered right down.  "The Aqua Nexus is still connected to the ocean floor.  We need to secure the seals and cut the connection.

"Of course.  Of course," said Leonidis, the excitement still in his voice.  "What next Brad?"

Brad looked around and studied the screens.

"That is all I got," said Brad.  "I don't understand any of these other symbols.  I would guess that until you take off, you won't be able to see what they mean or test them."

Leonidis got up from his chair and shook Brad's hand vigorously.

"You are an Atlantean, Sir. Thank you for your guidance in here today."

Seeing Leonidis excited with a big smile on his face was not something Brad expected. His joy was almost infectious.

"I was happy to help," said Brad. "I expect that as long as the three of you work in unison you will get to your destination soon."

Brad expected his comment to cool off Leonidis' excitement, but it didn't. He stepped out of the control room and raised his hands in the air. The men waiting for the Three cheered.

"Go, spread the word," ordered Leonidis. "Tomorrow we leave for home."

# Chapter 19

"Leonidis is here," John announced as Leonidis walked in behind him.

None of the MacIvers made any effort to move, but Iris got up to prepare tea.

"I did not expect to see you here, Helen."

Helen was in the MacIvers apartment not to see them, but to spend time with her husband. In his role as Iris' assistant, he was never far from her so for Helen that meant going where he was. She was happy to do so after not being able to see him for many years. John put one of his big hands gently on Helen's shoulder.

"Ah, of course," said Leonidis, as he found a place to sit. "I apologize for the intrusion Helen."

Iris handed a cup of tea to Leonidis and returned to her spot next to Brad, taking hold of his hand as she made herself comfortable.

"I just noticed your bracelets. Few in the city display such colors," commented Leonidis. "Forever and into the next life," he said, looking at Brad.

"Forever and into the next life," said Brad proudly.

Leonidis carried himself differently from his past visits. He was relaxed and even smiling. For some of the MacIvers, this seemed oddly suspicious, but Brad assumed it was carry over from the success they had in the control room.

"I have come to ask a favor, though seeing by your bracelets you have completed the ceremony, it may not be necessary."

Amar started to say something, but Antonia elbowed him in the ribs.

"I would like to ask if you, and your family, will stay with us a while longer. I think we could benefit from some more guidance on operating the controls, and if we have problems with the engines, you Kelly," said Leonidis as he looked at her kindly, "are the only person that seems to know how they operate."

"We have to go home," said Bjorn. "Our parents need us."

Leonidis nodded but waited for Brad to answer.

"What does Brad know about flying a spaceship?" blurted Amar. "And ceremony?"

"The controls are just like a video game," said Brad.

"Cool," said Amar.

"Iris and I have talked about this time a great deal," said Brad, a slight shake in his voice, but feeling Iris squeeze his hand gave him the strength to hold back his tears. "I will be returning to my home and fate will hopefully return me to Atlantis in the future."

Leonidis looked disappointed, but not surprised.

"As to how long we can remain here," said Brad. "That is in the hands of the person neither of us trust or wish to speak with.

Leonidis looked around the room and noticed Allen was not with them.

"I will get Allen," said Antonia.

As Antonia passed behind Brad she smacked her brother firmly on the back of the head. Leonidas looked at Brad curiously.

"Women in my culture are a force of their own," said Brad. "And I think my sister does not appreciate my reference to Allen."

"I don't think our opinion differs much," said Leonidis. "And with his actions, I suspect that women here will become a similar…force."

Allen entered the common area behind Antonia, but he did not move far beyond the hallway. He looked tired and worn down.

"We can stay until Atlantis passes beyond the ice and past the Thebe gossamer ring. We can stay no longer than that. Like Atlantis, we have a trajectory we must stay within or we will not arrive home."

Allen was deceiving the people around him again, and it hurt his soul, but he had to get his family home.

Leonidis sipped on his tea and thought about his next words. The MacIvers listened as he told Allen that he could understand if Allen thought he was trying to keep the MacIvers there because there would be obvious benefits. But he also believed that the Atlanteans would quickly turn against him, as they had recently, if they found out he did such a thing. His only concern now was for the safety of the people of Atlantis.

"Perhaps the people that pilot your ship could help us," said Leonidis.

"I pilot the ship," said Allen. "It responds to me, just as Atlantis responds to the Three. It is just more advanced than Atlantis so I do not need to have that direct connection."

Allen's eyes never diverted from Leonidis'. He was telling a lie that was obvious to his family and he could only hope that none of them revealed that.

"I am sorry," said Allen. "We have done all we can, and our time here has come to an end."

Allen turned and returned to his room.

"Perhaps we could allow him in the control room for a short time since he does have piloting knowledge," said Helen.

"No," said Leonidis, but not angrily. "Brad seems capable, and I do believe my distrust of the boy would distract me from controlling the ship."

"Allen," said Bjorn boldly. "Not the boy."

Helen did not have those same trust issues, but she could see how they would easily distract Leonidis. Leonidis rose from his seat and handed his teacup to Antonia.

"I thank you for your hospitality, Brad. I will be on my way. I am sure you have much to do on this last night."

Leonidis stopped and turned at the doorway.

"Brad. Iris. I will leave you with some words my grandfather often told us. I hope the translation carries them same meaning it does in my language." Leonidis paused and took a deep breath. "Life is too long to live unhappy, so find the people and the things that bring happiness into your life and keep them close. Life is also too short, so grasp the moments of happiness when they are there and hold them tight, for they may not pass your way again."

"Seeing you with your family, and with Iris, who is also your family now, I think you have embraced the first part, and I find myself jealous. Tonight do not forget the second part."

Leonidis left, and the room remained silent.

"I am not crying," said Deane as she got up and left the room.

"John, Brad will keep me safe tonight. It is a good night for you to walk your wife home," said Iris.

John bowed deeply, then took Helen by her hand and they left. Iris took Brad by the hand out to the deck.

"If any one of you go near that deck door tonight, Kelly's temper be nothing compared to what you see from me," said Antonia firmly. "Understand?"

All the MacIvers nodded their heads.

"I have questions, though," said Amar.

"No, you don't," said Sheila.

"Okay then. No, I don't."

# Chapter 20

Brad slipped a blanket over Iris as he slipped out of her arms. The lights of the city were just coming up and she had just fallen asleep. They had spent the night on the deck, talking about everything, and about nothing, and not talking at all but just holding each other close as they watched the creatures of the ocean. Brad did not sleep, not wanting to miss a single moment of the time he had left with Iris.

He had heard John enter the apartment earlier so he was comfortable stepping away from her. Brad walked across the hall and entered Iris' parent's apartment without ringing, in the Atlantean way. He walked out to the deck where he knew he would find Iris' father drinking tea and reading.

"Son," said Iris' father. "It is an unusual day we enter."

Iris' mother brought out tea for Brad and sat next to her husband.

"I don't know if I will have another chance to see you today," said Brad. "I wanted to say goodbye and thank you, for the help and understanding, and for your daughter. I won't apologize for how I have messed up her future because that would be to deny her feelings for me, and my feelings for her."

Brad sipped at his tea, wetting his mouth.

"I know that this may not be the Atlantean way, but if another man enters her life in my absence, do not deny her her happiness."

"There will be no other man," said Iris' father.

Brad assumed he was just holding to tradition.

"I respect you sir, but you can not know that."

Iris' father set his tablet down on the table in front of him so Brad could see what he was looking at. There were images of bracelets similar to Brad's.

"This one here is the same color as yours and my daughters. We have not seen that in many hundreds of years. The bond you two have goes beyond fate and love. Those colors say so," said Iris' father. "So, I do know that. There is not a doubt in my mind that you will return to her. But…if it gives you comfort, know that she will not be denied her happiness."

Brad shook his father's hand.

"Travel well, son"

Back at his apartment, Brad found Bjorn sitting in the common area.

"She is still asleep," said John, trying desperately to whisper with his booming voice. "I have sent the others back to their room so they would not wake her, but he refused."

Brad laughed and looked at his little brother, who was now standing beside him holding out a rolled-up paper. Brad unrolled the paper and felt his eyes burn, but he denied the tears. It was a beautiful sketch of that moment Brad got his first kiss, done with the detail and precision Bjorn took pride in.

"That is yours to bring home," said Bjorn. "This is for you to give to her."

Bjorn handed Brad a rolled-up canvas. Brad carefully unrolled it, and it was the same image in full color and perfect detail.

"You amaze me, little man. Thank you."

Brad handed the canvas to John.

"Keep this secret and safe until I ask for it but keep it with you."

Out on the deck, Brad stroked Iris' hair and kissed her to wake her. She shifted and opened her eyes and stared at Brad.

"This is the image I will wake to every morning in my heart."

The common area was fully occupied by MacIver kids when they entered from the deck. There was much commotion and conversation and laughter, but there was no Allen. He remained in his room, not wanting to dampen the spirits of his family. John brought him food, and even though he wasn't invited to, John sat on the floor across from Allen who was in his wheelchair.

"Do they make those things in my size?" asked John as he flicked a finger against the frame of the chair.

Allen shrugged.

"I haven't seen one, but I am sure they do," said Allen. "They even make them with their own engines so you don't have to push."

John broke a piece of fish in two and handed half to Allen.

"There are days when I am tired and don't breathe so well. Days I feel weak. I could use one of those.

"The radiation," said Allen. "It makes changes to you that will do that. We know about it, and we know what changes it makes, but we don't know how to reverse it when it is in a body too long."

John broke a biscuit and handed half to Allen, but Allen shook his head.

"Really!" said John. "These are my favorite. My mother could never keep enough of them in the house. Do you know what else makes changes to a person Allen?"

"Too many of those biscuits?"

John laughed loudly.

"Yes, that too. But hate changes a person. I don't think Brad hates you, he is just sad and angry. I remember feeling like that when I was sent away from Helen. But hate for yourself eats you up from the inside, just like this radiation stuff is doing to me."

John broke another piece of fish, giving Allen half as he stood up.

"Time to get going. We have places to be. I am going to grab a few more biscuits first."

———————————

Leonidis was watching them seal the base of the Aqua Nexus when Helen arrived.

"I have not heard you speak as well as you did last night, Leonidis," said Helen. "That was a beautiful sentiment you left Brad and Iris with."

"I do have a heart," said Leonidis, in a joking tone.

Helen wasn't so sure. During their walk home the previous night she and John were confronted by a horrific scene that no man with a heart could be part of, but she knew Leonidis had a hand in it.

"Did you see their bracelets?" Leonidis said excitedly. "I looked those colors up and there has only been one other instance of it in several generations. And the story of that union is one we have heard in myths and tales."

Iris arrived and was welcomed by Leonidis and Helen. Kelly and Brad were with her. They watched as the workers finished closing off the base of the Aqua Nexus. Leonidis was handed a button which he quickly pushed and the geothermal piping below them disconnected. The city moved as the piping came free and continued to move gently.

"Must be just enough water current to move the city," said Kelly.

"Well then we should get moving under our own power quickly," said Leonidis.

They made their way to the market square, where everyone in the city had gathered. Leonidis got up on a table to make an announcement. When Helen was sure he was completely distracted she pulled Iris aside and whispered in her ear. Iris' hand moved to cover her mouth in shock, but Helen stopped her and continued whispering. Leonidis did not notice as he had the crowd's full attention.

"We are about to leave this ocean and make our way home. Something generations of Atlanteans have dreamed of doing. The last time our great city moved was, well yesterday."

There was a roar of laughter from the crowd.

"But it has been thousands of years since the city crashed into this ocean. We do not know what will happen," said Leonidis seriously. "We do not know what dangers lie ahead. But just as we came together over the last couple of days to protect our people from radiation, we will come together again when needed."

The crowd cheered and Leonidis waited for them to go quiet again.

"Until we are free from these waters, remain together and keep each other safe."

Leonidis stepped down from the table with the help of his men. As he did a man started the chant they had heard the day before. A woman joined in, and then the crowd joined. It was an amazing, moving sound to hear.

The Three, joined by Kelley and Brad, and their assistants, made their way through the crowd to the Aqua Nexus. When they arrived at the up top level Brad expected to find several of Leonidis' men there along with his sons, but there was nobody. Helen and Leonidis had each only brought one assistant with them, and each of them, along with John, positioned themselves outside one of the three doorways to the control room.

Each of the Three sat down in their chair, Iris taking a moment to kiss Brad before she sat down. The chair arms did their thing, and the chairs themselves adjusted to the bodies in them as if the ship knew there was a long trip ahead.

"Iris, you had the most accurate control of the power. I think it would be best if you managed that," said Leonidis. "Just like we finished up yesterday."

"What about the ice?" asked Kelly. "Do we just crash through it?"

"As an engineer, you will like this," said Leonidis. "I have been reading and studying the texts since I was a child. If the theory is correct, we will barely feel a bump. So we want just enough power to tap the bottom of the ice, Iris."

Leonidis looked at Helen and Iris.

"Are you not excited? I truly am. Let's begin."

The power on the engines fired up and Iris added more bit by bit. Leonidis directed the power and the gentle thrumming filled the ship as it lifted from the ocean floor and began to move upward. As it did more images appeared on the screens.

"I can't tell if we are moving," said Iris. "All I see is water."

Brad pointed at one of her screens.

"Look here. I think this dot is us and this solid area up here is the ice. Give it a little more gas."

"Gas?" questioned Iris.

"He means power," said Kelly.

Iris increased the power and the dot moved towards the sold mass quicker.

"Ease up. Ease Up," said Brad.

Iris let the power go down to almost nothing and the dot's progress slowed. She played with the power a little, getting a feel for it. As the dot neared the solid mass on the screen, Iris let off the power completely. The ship continued to move up but also sideways. It felt like it was tipping. Iris gave it a little power and the other two tried to balance it between all engines. The ship continued up but at an angle.

"This. This," said Brad as he tapped an image on Leonidis' screen. "You want that level."

He tapped the image on Helen's screen.

"This one."

Leonidis and Helen worked surprisingly well together directing the power until that line was level, and according to the other image, the ship was moving straight up again.

From their seats the Three could see through the peak of the dome and a light glow filled their view.

"That's it. That is the surface," said Helen.

"Move carefully," said Leonidis.

The Three talked back and forth. They had reverted to their language, forgetting that Brad and Kelly were there. Brad reached for the wall to steady himself as the ship jolted. He looked up and could see they were against the ice.

"Raise the power," Leonidis directed Iris.

She did and the ship rocked from side to side. Leonidis and Helen worked to keep the ship pointed straight up."

"That is genius," said Kelly as she watched overhead.

She ran out of the control room to look out the sides of the dome and then back in.

"I told you so," said Leonidis.

Kelly could see that Leonidis was speaking to her, but she didn't understand a word. Leonidis realized he was speaking Atlantean and changed back to English.

"I told you so," he repeated.

"What is happening?" asked Brad.

Kelly explained how they were using the engines to heat the water. That hot water was rising and heating the outside of the dome and the ice above them. They were melting their way through the ice with almost no stress on the dome.

From the market square, the Atlanteans watched as the dome eased into the ice. The ice worked its way further and further down the sides of the dome. Some held each other close as they watched nervously, while others cheered. Others tried not to watch at all, finding other things to distract them.

The MacIver kids watched the event unfold from the observation deck where they had first entered the dome. Iris' parents had brought them there so they could watch it away from the crowd. Two men approached them.

"Have you seen Diana?"

Allen recognized them as Leonidis' sons.

"I don't know who Diana is," said Allen.

"Their sister," said Iris' father.

"Oh, I have never met her," said Allen. "I don't know what she looks like."

"Can we help you look for her," offered Antonia.

"No, no, no. She is probably just in the crowd somewhere.

The two men left as quickly as they came.

———————————

"Is that sky?" asked Brad.

At the peak of the dome was an expanding spot of blackness.

"Easy," said Leonidis. Let the heat do the work."

---

There was silence in the market square. The Atlanteans watched stars appear above them. Real stars. This was the first sky any Atlantean had seen in thousands of years.

---

"So cool," said Amar as he laid on his back and watched the top of the dome.

Bjorn quickly sketched trying to lock the image in his memory.

Iris' father pulled his wife close and kissed her. It was the first real affection any of the MacIvers had seen between them.

---

"Let's bring it to the edge of that circle," said Leonidis. He was quickly grasping the information on the screens in front of him.

"Then we will let the power off and drift. I think we all would like to look back at the place we have lived for so long."

Iris waited, breathing deeply, waiting until the ice was at the widest part of the dome, and then she boosted the power to three-quarters. The Three were sucked back in their seats and Brad and Kelly fell to the floor. Iris panicked and stopped all power and watched the screen as the ship drifted upwards, surprisingly settling at the edge of the white circle.

Leonidis stared intently at Iris. She prepared for him to start yelling at her. What she got instead was laughter. Loud belly laughter. Leonidis said something in Atlantean in between his laughter and the other two joined in. Kelly and Brad just looked at each other and shrugged. Brad noticed something on the screens that was new.

"What do you think this is?" asked Brad.

The Three looked at their screens and studied them.

"That would be the route to our final destination," said Helen.

Leonidis' eyes opened wide.

"You are right!"

Leonidis got out of his chair and invited the others to join him. They walked to the side of the dome and far below them they could see the moon that held their people captive for so long.

---

People in the marketplace picked themselves off the floor and then helped others. They slowly made their way to the side of the dome and looked at the moon below them and the sky around them.

---

Allen reached for Dean to help her up. Amar was helping the others. He was already on his back when the ship took off, so he didn't fall. Iris' mother didn't fall either and helped steady her husband so he didn't.

"Floor walker legs, I think," she answered when Amar asked why she didn't fall. "We get bounced around pretty good in the currents sometimes."

"I don't think you are going to be walking in any ocean for a while said Bjorn as he pointed at Europa.

"Wait a minute. Why aren't we all floating," asked Amar.

"Like our ship," said Allen. "It must have its own gravity."

# Chapter 21

From their position, the icy surface of Europa stretched beneath like a cracked canvas of ethereal whites and pale blues. Jagged fractures formed intricate patterns across the landscape, resembling the delicate veins of an otherworldly marble.

The surface was pocked with craters, reflecting the distant sunlight in an almost crystalline manner. Vast regions of the moon were covered in a network of interconnected lines, reminiscent of frozen rivers etched into the icy surface.

A plume of water vapor rose from the moon's surface, escaping the subterranean ocean below. It reached up like ghostly tendrils, catching the light before dissipating into the vacuum of space.

"That must have been where Atlantis broke through the ice," someone commented.

Beyond Europa another of Jupiter's moons was visible.

Ganymede seemed unimpressive in the distance and attracted little attention from the Atlanteans, who felt like they were leaving something precious behind under the ice of Europa.

The thrumming filled the air again and Atlantis moved away from Europa. As Europa moved into the distance, everyone's attention was drawn to the massive orb that looked as though it were made from bands of swirling, hypnotic colors.

---

In the control room, the Three had returned to their seats. Brad and Kelly along with the Three assistants remained at the side of the dome watching the skies outside.

The Three carefully navigated Atlantis away from Europa, following a trajectory that had been input into the ship before it crashed into the moon. They could see Jupiter on their screen and through their dome, but panic was setting in for Leonidis as no matter what they did the ship seemed to be drifting towards Jupiter.

"We can't let this happen again," said Leonidis.

The Three attempted several different movements but they only seemed to drift towards the mass of swirling clouds faster.

"Sir," said Iris gently. "You have led the way to us leaving the ocean to find our way home. We can tell that you are invested in getting us there safe, and as is your nature you will do that by sheer will if necessary."

Leonidis took his eyes off his screens to look at Iris. She could see the anger surfacing in him.

"That was not meant as a criticism, but as respect," Iris quickly added "I only wish to suggest that force alone may not be enough to stop this fall."

Leonidis calmed himself and looked across to Helen.

"I think she is right. In this moment perhaps Iris should lead us," said Helen calmly.

Leonidis rested his head against the back of his chair and closed his eyes. He breathed deeply to calm himself because he had realized what the others had already seen, that his emotions affected his ability to control the ship.

"Tell me what I should do," said Leonidis. "But know that we are falling into the den of the dragon."

John and the other two assistants looked at each other strangely. Kelly caught their look. John explained that they were falling into those clouds and that Leonidis was letting Iris lead them away safely. Brad and Kelly had heard the discussion in the control room but didn't understand anything that was being said.

"You should be in there, Brad," said Kelly.

"No," said Brad. "Iris has got this."

---

Everyone watched with fascination as they got closer and closer to Jupiter. They could see the bands of clouds streak across Jupiter's face, each layer boasting its own distinct hue. Deep browns, rusty reds, and ochres swirled around and through each other. Amid all the turmoil a giant, swirling, crimson-red spot stood out on its own, as though all the other clouds were avoiding it.

"Do you think they really saw a dragon in there?" asked Bjorn.

"There may still be a dragon in there," said Iris' father. "But I hope we don't find out."

"Cool," said Amar as he lay back down to watch the skies.

"I suggest we all do what Amar is," Allen said calmly as he locked the brakes on his wheelchair.

———————————

Looking out of the dome you couldn't tell what was happening, but from their seats in the control room, the Three could see that Atlantis was moving faster and faster towards Jupiter without any help from the engines of the Atlantis. Leonidis called to his assistant, giving him directions, and the assistant bolted away. He did not stop running until he reached people on the edge of the city.

"Sit down. Hold on," he yelled, as he tried to catch his breath between words.

From their position on the observation deck, the

MacIvers could see a wave of motion radiate around the edges of the city and the Atlanteans found places on the ground and objects to take hold of. In the control room, the Three made minor adjustments to the ship, letting it continue to hurtle toward the planet but aiming Atlantis for the side of the giant planet.

"Just like the game children play with beads," said Iris.

Helen and Leonidis nodded. John wrapped his massive arms around Kelly and Brad and Helen's assistant sat on the floor, taking hold of a column. The gentle thrum changed to a scream as the city shook. Iris used all her will to raise and keep the power at maximum. Helen and Leonidis strained to keep Atlantis pointed away from Jupiter. The Atlantis raced away from Jupiter and Atlanteans watched with fear as they skimmed by Io.

Iris dropped the power, removing her arms from their gauntlets.

"I am sorry," she cried. "I did not think about that moon being in our path."

Helen got out of her chair and went over to comfort Iris. Helen was sweaty and shaking herself. Leonidis watched them but remained in his chair watching his screens.

"I think you did exactly what was needed," said Leonidis, the calmness in his voice hiding the fear he felt only moments before.

"I think it was the exact same thing they did when they approached Jupiter thousands of years ago. There was no dragon. Did you not see the flames shroud us as we got close to that planet? That was their dragon!" said Leonidis. "Fate was in our favor, unlike our ancestors who did not miss the moon in front of them."

Leonidis watched a small object approach them on his screen, and they felt a shudder in the city.

"It would seem that it is time for our guests to leave."

He called Brad and Kelly over.

"I would shake your hand, Sir," but I think it best one of us continues to watch these screens. "We are grateful for the help you and your family have provided us and you are always welcome back. You are Atlantean."

He motioned with his head to the top of the dome and in the distance they could see the moon Callisto.

"You will have to say your goodbyes before we pass that point."

As they exited the Aqua Nexus, John separated and went off in another direction from them. Hellen guided them quickly through the city, and Iris held tightly to Brad's hand. Brad hoped that John had not forgotten about the item he held for him. When they arrived at the observation platform Allen was not there. He had already boarded the ship. There was no crowd or fanfare. The Atlanteans were occupied with the new future they faced and were not even aware that the ship the MacIvers were waiting for had arrived.

Antonia, who had entered the ship with Allen was coming back out to the observation deck as the last of the MacIvers said hugged everyone, and made his way to the ship, leaving Brad behind. Brad was surprised to see Antonia coming off the ship. In her hand, she carried something that was moving.

"I thought John would be with you." Said Antonia.

"He will be along shortly," said Helen. "You should see the view from the city level," Helen added as she looked at Iris' parents.

They took the hint. They had already said their goodbyes so Iris' father shook Brad's hand one last time and they returned home. Brad was relieved to hear that John would be along shortly. Antonia handed Helen the object in her hand and Helen almost dropped it when it moved.

"That is a gift for the Atlanteans. Place it near one of your engines and in time you will have enough to cover all of the engines. You will not have to worry about radiation leaks again."

"Thank you," said Helen as she held the creature up to get a closer look at it.

John arrived, gasping for air. He carried a large bag over his shoulder.

"I was not built for speed."

Everyone laughed and John started to join them when he was surprised by Antonia jabbing him with something. He looked at her oddly.

"It is medicine, John," said Antonia. "I do not know if it will cure you, but I am told it will ensure you have a long life with your lovely wife. Allen said to tell you that you will never have to worry about a wheelchair."

"Thank you," said John. "Can I follow you into your ship to drop off this bag?"

"I am sorry, but you can't come in. But I can carry that in for you."

John laughed.

"Can I carry it as far as the door, and Brad can carry it the rest of the way."

"Sure," said Antonia, curious about what could be in the bag.

John set the bag down just outside the door and hugged Antonia, lifting her off her feet. Antonia entered the ship and John returned to stand beside his wife. He reached inside his tunic and handed Brad the rolled-up canvas as he bowed.

"It has been an honor, my friend."

"As it has been for me, John. I have one last favor to ask," said Brad.

"You do not have to ask," said John as he reached out to shake Brad's hand. "I will keep her safe. Carry that bag in gently."

"Come, my dear," John said to Helen. "We are not needed here."

Helen bowed to Brad, and he returned the gesture.

Brad looked at the painting in his hand and then handed it to Iris. She unrolled it, and though she promised herself she would not, she cried.

"That was my first kiss," said Brad.

Iris embraced Brad and kissed him passionately.

"There will never be a last kiss for us, my love," she whispered in his ear. "We will see each other again."

Brad touched his bracelet to hers and felt the tone in his body.

"I believe that now, my love."

Iris handed Brad a folded-up piece of paper but stopped him from opening it up. "You are not to read it until your ship pulls away."

"Forever and into the next life," said Brad as he held Iris close one last time. "I love you."

"Forever and into the next life," said Iris. "My love for you shall stay true."

Iris watched as Brad walked to the ship. He struggled to lift the bag John had set down, but he was careful to be gentle with it as John told him to be. The door closed behind as soon as he entered the ship. Iris lost her composure and her legs felt weak. It was only the feel of John's hand on her shoulder that kept her standing. She leaned into the big man and cried. She felt Atlantis shudder as the MacIver ship disconnected and she cried more.

# Chapter 22

Brad unfolded the note the moment he set the bag down.

*My love, I wish that I could return with you to your home, but we know that cannot be. But I know your heart, and trust that who I am sending with you, will be cared for and protected by your family and as her brother, you will care for her as you would me. Keep her safe. She would never be safe here.*

*We shall be together again soon.*

*Forever and into the next life.*

Brad read the note a couple of times, trying to comprehend what Iris was telling him. Then he quickly dropped to a knee and opened the bag. The battered and bruised face of a girl stared back at him from inside the bag.

"Move," said Antonia, pushing Brad back.

She quickly opened the bag and helped the girl out of it.

Joane helped as they guided her to a chair.  Pinqua observed from across the room.

"Diana?" Brad questioned, barely able to recognize the girl he had met a few days ago.

"Diana, as in Leonidis' daughter Diana?" asked Sheila.

Brad shrugged. Antonia looked at the girl in front of her gently.

"Is that who you are?"

The girl nodded.

"Your brothers were looking for you.  We need to get you back."

"No," the girl's voice cracked.  Fear filled her eyes. "They did this to me.  They helped my father do this to me."

"She is not going back," said Brad firmly.  "Iris has said she is to be a MacIver, so she is."

Allen watched from across the room as Antonia treated the girl's injuries with help from her sisters.  Pinqua brought in items for them to use.  She had two very black eyes and a bloodied bruise around her neck.  Bruises in the shape of handprints were on her arms and one arm was twisted in an awkward direction.  Antonia spoke quietly to Piqua and with of few touches of his control panel a wall formed separating the girls, leaving Brad, Allen, Bjorn, and Amar standing awkwardly on the other side of the wall.  Pinqua joined them.

"Will she be okay," asked Brad.

"Physically her body will recover," said Pinqua. "We cannot travel at speed until her injuries are cared for."

Pinqua touched a panel and a large window appeared in front of them. They could see the Atlantis just ahead of them, and their ship seemed to be keeping pace. Brad strained his eyes to see if he could see Iris in her chair.

"Why did you ask us to save people like that," said Amar. "People that would do that to their daughter and sister.

"Because it is my people that removed them from their home world and changed how they developed," said Pinqua.

Long before his time, his people shared a planet with the Atlanteans and the Loma. Pinqua's people went to war with the Loma, though who started the war and over what was not clear. In the process of war, they destroyed the planet's ability to support life. Pinqua's people had won in the end but gained nothing. The war had not only destroyed the planet but most of the third race, the Atlanteans, who were innocent bystanders.

Pinqua's people, like the Loma, had the ability to leave the planet and travel elsewhere, but the Atlanteans did not have that technology. Whether it was out of guilt and remorse, or as compensation, Pinqua's people built the Atlantis. They included many safeguards because they had just bore witness to what rampant technological advances could result in, and they sent them to Earth. When the ship left Earth it should have returned to its home planet.

"So, they are returning to a dead planet," said Brad.

"No," said Pinqua. "Planet X and your people call it, I mean the people of Earth, not Atlantis, is a thriving planet now. It has recovered over the many thousands of years. And when Atlantis sets down there, the city will never fly again."

Pinqua seemed to hear a sound and with a touch of his screen, the wall dropped. Diana looked better, but still not well. She got up from her chair and walked to Brad, Joane staying close by her side to steady her. Joane took Brad's hand and placed a vial in it.

"What is this?"

"You," said Diane. "Part of you that I stole from you."

Diana faltered and Joane guided her into a nearby chair.

"We have technology that most Atlanteans don't know about. We can use it to make a baby using parts of a person like the skin and hair that is in that tube," said Diana, her voice getting stronger as she spoke.

"My father's plan for me to have your child never changed, even after you claimed Iris. He was going to use that, and contributions from my brothers to create a child that had the genetics of both lines of two lines of the Three. I was to be the carrier of that child."

Brad sat down to hear the rest, as did the other MacIvers.

When Diana refused her father became violent with her. He beat her and had her brothers hold her down while the doctor prepared the samples from the vials. If they hadn't been interrupted by someone, she would never have got away, but she did. It was only by luck that she ran into John and Helen in the streets that night. They took her to their home and hid her. It was Helen's idea for her to leave with the MacIvers and her plan on how to sneak her onto their ship.

"Do not blame Iris for me being here," said Diana.

"I don't," said Brad. "She did the right thing."

"It is time to leave," said Pinqua.

"Do we have to sleep this time," asked Bjorn as he stared out the window.

"You don't," said Pinqua, "but you will."

Diana fell asleep immediately. Some of the others joined her, and while everyone else fought sleep, the excitement of the day waned, and with that, their energy, and they too fell asleep. All except Allen. Allen remained sitting in his wheelchair, watching the stars pass them by.

"It was a difficult decision," said Pinqua as he stood beside Allen. "I wish I could tell you that they will get easier, but I can not."

"Can I not tell them? Warn them so they can prepare?" asked Allen.

"No."

They stood together watching the stars quietly.

"Will he see her again?" asked Allen.

"Yes," said Pinqua.

Allen felt a sense of relief.

# Chapter 23

The Atlantis passed Callisto with the Three sitting in their seats.  They picked up speed as they passed Juno and with a little bit of work, they lined themselves up with the trajectory line that showed them the way home.  They felt the ship bounce a little when they crossed over the line and all of their screens lit up, then the gauntlets on all three of their chairs retracted.  Nothing shut down, despite none of the Three being directly connected.

"You have to see this," said John who was waiting with the other assistants outside of the control room.  The walls on the exterior of the control room had come to life as screens and control panels revealed themselves.

"Auto-pilot," said Iris quietly.

"What was that?" asked Helen.

Iris got up from her chair and walked around the control room.

"Brad told me about something called autopilot that ships have.  It is like the computer drives the ship when the real pilots need a rest, or when it is long and safe.  He says someone just needs to watch for trouble in case the pilot is needed."

Leonidis was outside the control room now, looking at the screens on the outside of the control room walls and touching the control panels.  "They can watch from out here.  These are like science stations.  They show some of what we see inside, and stuff that we don't need to see to fly the ship."

Helen and Iris joined Leonidis and Helen followed his lead.  She played with one of the consoles while Leonidis played with another.

"Look," she said, "That is the planet that almost sucked us in, and that is the moon we were living on."

She tapped the console and the image zoomed out.

"95 moons.  That planet has 95 moons."

"I think we should invite some of our scientists and engineers up here to monitor these screens and document what they find," said Leonidis as he looked at Iris.

"I agree," said Iris.  Helen nodded.

"Those are your people, Helen," said Leonidis.  "Go and find the right people and assign the tasks.  There should always be people here.  I am going to go home and see how my children are doing."

"I will stay until we have workers here," said Iris.

Leonidis left quickly. Helen called her assistant, and they went down to the city to recruit workers. Iris found a place to sit on the floor, leaning up against the dome. From her spot, she could see the big screens, see out the side of Atlantis, and see the vastness of the space around them. She motioned for John to join her. John joined her on the floor, getting down in a manner that was nowhere near as graceful as Iris had.

"I have a problem," said Iris. "I find myself alone while Brad is absent. I can not return to my parents because that would not be appropriate. Nor is my living alone. I would like to invite you and Helen to live with me. That way you are always there as my assistant, and nearby to protect me as I am sure Brad asked you."

Iris looked at John to see his reaction and his smile confirmed that Brad did ask him to watch over her.

"It will let me follow our cultural standards. And you get to live with your wife once again because your work with me won't be keeping you absent from her."

"We would like that very much, I think. Though I will have to ask Helen. I was worried you were going to ask me about something else."

"There is nothing else, John," said Iris firmly. "We agreed that it never happened."

John nodded his head and looked out at the stars. An older man and a young woman stepped off the elevator.

"We were sent by Helen," said the young woman.

Iris motioned at the glowing panels.

"Pick your spot, but please do not enter the control room."

---

"What do you mean you can't find her," screamed Leonidis. "We live inside a domed city with all the exits closed."

Leonidis' son cowered as his father yelled and threw things.

"Where is that useless brother of yours?"

"He is checking the places we have used in the past to … hide things."

Leonidis stared his son down.

"She would have to be dead to be there, and we did not kill her," screamed Leonidis.

"You hit her pretty hard…"

Leonidis spun on his heels and punched his son firmly in the stomach. His son fell over and vomited.

"Was it that hard?" Leonidis screamed. "Did I hit her that hard? You're not dead!"

Leonidis paced the room.

"Besides, who would have put her there if they found her dead in the streets? We would have heard if someone found her in any condition."

Leonidis' son struggled to his feet.

"That meddling boy didn't take her, did he?" asked Leonidis.

His son shook his head.

"Speak up," Leonidis yelled, spittle flying from his mouth.

"No. We watched every one of them get on that ship. It was only the MacIvers. Diana was not there."

"If anyone comes looking for her, she is sick," said Leonidis. "Very sick. We think she was exposed to the radiation."

"Yes, sir," his son said.

"Clean that mess up off the floor," Leonidis said as he left the room.

A MacIver Kids Adveture by Lawrence Nault

# Chapter 24

Pinqua's ship had been settled on Earth for a while when the MacIvers woke up. Pinqua had landed in the same location they had left from. It was late at night but the MacIvers felt like it was morning.

"Your bodies have become accustomed to an Atlantean day, which has somehow become a much longer day than it was when they lived on Earth. Not seeing a sun or stars must have something to do with that."

"Doesn't Jupiter have a shorter day," asked Amar. "Like ten hours or something."

His brothers and sisters looked at him strangely.

"What. I pay attention in class sometimes," said Amar.

"Cool," said Bjorn in a mocking voice, mimicking Amar's standard response.

They all laughed, which woke Diana. Diana sat up quickly and searched the room nervously.

"You are safe," said Antonia.

"We need to figure out what we are going to tell people about her," said Brad.

"I will deal with that," said Allen.

Brad shook his head.

"I don't think so."

Sheila stepped in.

"Brad, we all have our own skills, and I think this is something Allen might be a little more successful at."

"If you mean lying, you are probably right," said Brad. "Fine."

Pinqua wouldn't let the MacIvers leave the ship. He showed on his screen the dots that were people hiding in the woods and a drone that circled the area.

"There will be more people on the trails when they open the gates in the morning," said Pinqua. "You can blend in then."

"I don't think we will blend in wearing these," said Bjorn, tugging at the Atlantean clothes they were wearing.

Diana pointed to the bag that was still on the floor.

"Iris used your old clothes for padding so I wouldn't get hurt," she said.

Antonia rooted through the bag, tossing the boys their clothes.

"Come with us, Diana."

Diana joined the girls, and Pinqua touched his screen so they were behind a wall again. When the wall came down the girls were dressed, and Diana was still wearing her Atlantean clothes, but with many accessories, so she looked like a model off a magazine cover.

"You look beautiful," said Brad.

"You are part of a union and should not speak in such a way to a woman," said Diana.

Brad pulled the note Iris gave him out of his pocket and showed it to Diana.

"You see that," said Brad, pointing at the note. "As a brother. I am your brother."

Diana laughed, which was good to see. She read the note a couple of times before handing it back.

"Iris is amazing. You are a lucky man."

"Yes, I am," said Brad as he carefully folded the note and put it back in his pocket.

"You do look quite beautiful," said Allen, "But if anyone asks about the bruises on your face, I would suggest saying you tripped and fell. Amar's face looked like that when he fell down the stairs."

"Leave it to you to find the perfect lie," said Brad.

"That's enough Brad," said Kelly. "More than enough."

Brad walked away, as far as he could within the confines of the ship.

The trails filled up with people on bikes, jogging, and some just out for a walk on what was a beautiful morning. As a group passed nearby the door to the ship opened and the MacIvers quickly exited. Diana pushed Allen's wheelchair, not because Allen needed help, but because it provided her with some stability. As soon as they were out the door closed behind them and they were greeted by barking. Diana jumped back as a creature raced towards her and jumped into Allen's lap. She realized quickly that it wasn't dangerous.

"What is that?" she asked.

"This is a Fritter," said Allen. "A dog. A basset hound. And a donut stealer."

Diana tentatively reached out to touch the dog, and Fritter eagerly licked her hand.

"You need to stay on the trails," said a man none of the MacIvers recognized.

"Sorry, sir," said Allen. "My dog got away from me."

Baba appeared on the trail behind the strange man.

"Oh good, you found her," said Baba. "I was sure I closed that gate."

The man looked at Baba, and then at the MacIvers, and shook his head before walking away. Amar ran up and hugged his grandfather. Some of the MacIvers raced home while others just walked. Allen was at the back of the pack, as Diana pushed him along slowly beside Baba, with Fritter in his lap.

"I wasn't sure I was going to make it up here," said Baba. "My longest walk yet. Who is this lovely young lady you have brought back with you?"

"This is your niece. She has come to Canada to take care of you since you have been sick."

"Is that so," said Baba. "And what is my niece's name."

"I am Diana."

Nani was waiting on the deck when they got to the gate to the yard.

"You crazy old man! You walked up that hill!"

She would have kept going but she saw Diana pushing Allen's wheelchair. In the house Nani helped Baba sit, mumbling about him being a stubborn, stupid old man. Then she walked up to Diana, taking her chin in her hand and turning Diana's head from side to side.

"I hope you hit him with a truck," said Nani. "May he be cursed with hemorrhoids and be forced to ride a camel everywhere."

"Who is she," Nani asked, turning to Allen.

"Do you not recognize your niece who has traveled so far to help you take care of that stupid old man?

Nani shook her hand at Allen.

"You be careful Allen MacIver, or your food will be the spiciest on the table and your backside will pay the price."

Baba choked as he laughed.

"Is he looking for her?  That animal that did this?"

"He is not.  Nobody is."

Nana looked at Allen, then past him at the rest of the MacIvers sitting on the steps watching.  She turned and hugged Diana.

"Welcome.  I am glad you came.  I can use some help with this stupid old man."

Diana was a little overwhelmed but laughed at Nani's obviously loving reference to Baba.

"Toni, take her upstairs and find her some clothes. Look online for some more clothes for her.  I saved up some money not feeding you."

"You will stay here until their parents come home, then you will come and stay with Babi and me. It will be much quieter there," said Nani. "I don't even know your name yet."

"Diana."

"Diana. A beautiful name," said Nani. "Toni, if she needs anything else. Anything. We will get it for her. I have a friend from India. She used to be a doctor over there."

Antonia hugged Nani, then took Diana upstairs, the rest of the MacIver girls following along.

"There is chai ready, and I will warm up food. I have a feeling I am in for some tall tales," Nani said as she motioned to the boys and Allen to follow her into the kitchen.

When the girls came downstairs, Bjorn had his sketches laid out on the table. Nani was looking at the sketches as Bjorn eagerly described what he was showing them. The girls found their seats and Nani told Bjorn to put his pictures away as she put out food. Sheila realized that Diana had not followed them into the kitchen and went looking for her. She found Diana sitting in the front room with Baba. Baba was describing his son, Amar's father, in great detail.

"I am sorry," said Diana. "I have not seen him. Your family here are the first people to come to us that I know of."

Baba rocked in his chair.

"Did you want to come here with them?"

"I did," said Diana. "They are good people."

Baba rocked in his chair some more.

"Do your parents know you are here?"

"My mother got ill and passed away a long time ago. My father does not know."

"I think my son is like you. I think he went with good people to have a new, exciting life."

Baba's head bobbed as he nodded off. Diana put a blanket over him.

"I think you might be right," said Diana quietly.

"You are going to fit in just perfectly," said Sheila.

# Chapter 25

Allen sat in the yard looking up at the night sky. Fritter was in his lap. She had not gone far from him since he returned home. His family was still inside sharing stories.

"Can I join you two?"

Allen looked up to see Diana.

"That would be nice."

Diana sat down on the grass, running her fingers through the blades of grass in wonder. Fritter jumped out of Allen's lap and flopped down beside Diana, resting her chin on Diana's leg. Diana pet her the way she had seen Allen do, and she looked up at the sky too. Allen pointed at the sky.

"You see those couple of stars right there. We were somewhere right between them."

Diana pretended to know which stars he was pointing at. It didn't matter to her. They were all so beautiful.

"We came so far, so fast," said Diana. "I am here in this paradise, and it will be many, many years before Atlantis arrives at their home."

Allen looked down from the sky to Diana. She didn't take her eyes off the sky.

"I was not quite asleep when you were talking with that…Alien is what the others call it."

"Pinqua," said Allen.

"You carry a heavy load," said Diana. "And you can't even talk to your family about it. I can kind of understand because I have never in my life been able to talk about the realities of my life. I wanted to say that I will listen to your words and keep them close."

"I would like that," said Allen. "But I do not think Brad would approve. Truth is you would be better off to distance yourself from me. I seem to ruin lives."

"I don't think I understand."

"Baba was a spry old man until I got him involved in this and the Loma attacked him. Brad found someone he could share himself with, and I made it so they couldn't be together."

Diana didn't respond. She just looked at the sky.

"What is wrong with your legs," she asked out of nowhere.

"Nobody knows," says Allen. "None of the doctors could find a problem so I just accepted it and learned to deal with it.

"Your sister has told me that things are different here. That men don't control or claim women. That we can choose what we want to do. And they said women can do anything a man can do if they want to," said Diana. "Then, while we looked for clothes online, they showed me all these men. Movie stars and singing stars I think they call them. Stars seems like a strange word to use to describe people."

Allen laughed.

"It is a long way for me to say that I am going to take your sisters at their word," said Diana. "I am here, and I know things, even if it is by accident. So, I expect you to talk to me when you need to, because you are wrong about ruining lives and about yourself. I don't know what your sisters see in all those star people, but I am inserting myself into your life, and like your legs, you should just learn to deal with it and accept it."

Diana got up off the grass and headed into the house. Fritter followed her. Allen didn't know what to say. All he got out was "You're a traitor Fritter." The basset hound ignored him.

"You should come in and be with your family," Diana called back as she continued walking away.

"It might be better if you stayed away from him," said Brad as Diana climbed the stairs to the deck.

"I am going to speak to you as a sister, a sister from this planet," said Diana.

"Okay," said Brad cautiously.

"I know you are hurt. I know you are angry, but you should step back and try to see things from Allen's perspective. He is hurting too."

The door to the house burst open.

"Moms on the phone," yelled Bjorn. "Come talk to her."

He was back in the house as quickly as he came out. Brad followed him in. Allen worked his way across the lawn and up the ramp, moving slower than he usually did.

The MacIvers listened to their mother rant for 10 minutes about how they were never around when she called, and how they should be home more often. Then they listened for another ten minutes to her tell them about their grandmother and how she was doing and what all their relatives were up to. Then she said she had to go because she had so much to do and with a quick goodbye she hung up. The MacIver kids looked at each other and laughed.

"Were we supposed to get a chance to get some words in?" asked Bjorn.

Nani laughed.

"Every call has been like that. I think your mother is trying to fit years into a few weeks."

The kids were quickly off to bed. Diana joined Antonia in her room. There was surprisingly little talking. They were all tired. Brad sat in his bed, looking at the picture Bjorn had drawn of him and Iris while playing with this bracelet. He closed his eyes, and he could feel the vibrations from the bracelet flow through him, even though he only imagined hearing the tone. He cried. Silently he let the tears flow that he had been holding back. He wanted to hit someone or break something, but he couldn't, so he cried. Allen did this to him. He fell asleep sitting there, crying.

In his room, Allen could hear Brad, and feel Brad. Allen cried in silence with him and for him.

Diane touched her face and neck and arms and flinched with each touch. The MacIver girls had helped her to hide some of the bruises with clothes, and makeup for the bruises clothes didn't cover. It didn't change the fact they were there and every time she closed her eyes, she relived the beating she received. She was afraid to sleep. Antonia was sound asleep beside her. Carefully and quietly, Diana got up and went downstairs.

Allen heard a light knock on his door and quickly wiped the tears from his eyes. He saw Diana's head poke in the door.

"Would it be inappropriate for me to come in?" she asked quietly.

Allen motioned for her to come in.

"Just leave the door open a little."

Diana sat down on the floor and leaned back against the wall on the opposite side of the room from Allen.

"I am afraid to sleep," said Diana. "I am afraid to close my eyes. My father and brothers chase me in my dreams."

Allen just listened.

"You can feel it, can't you? The fear."

Allen nodded.

"Can you take it away or make it go away."

"No," said Allen sadly. "I think that kind of fear becomes part of you until you change it into something else.

Allen grabbed one of his pillows and tossed it to Diana, along with one of the blankets off his bed.

"But I will always listen to you, so you will just have to deal with it and learn to accept it."

Diana laughed, covering her mouth so she didn't wake anybody.

"Close your eyes and I will stand guard."

Diana laid down and pulled the blanket over herself. She closed her eyes and sleep found her. Allen was true to his word. He stayed awake and stood guard until he knew she was asleep, then he let himself fall asleep.

Nani was surprised to see Diana sitting at the kitchen table when she came downstairs the next morning.

I was hoping to join you at the market so I could learn about your foods.

Nani laughed.  She knew what Diana meant because in her childhood in India, she used to go to the street market every morning to shop for fresh food.  She pulled open the pantry doors and Diana was shocked.

"We don't have to go anywhere, but I will show you how to make the food if you like."

Diana nodded and happily joined Nani in cooking the breakfast and learning the names of the foods.  When Baba came downstairs and sat in his chair, Diana brought him in his morning chai.

"I am not used to service with a smile from a beautiful woman in the morning," said Baba.

Diana set the cup down on the table beside his chair.

"Did you enjoy your walk yesterday?"

"I did, but it was tiring."

"Can we go for a walk today? We don't have to go far. I would just like to see more."

"Yes, I think I would enjoy that."

The MacIvers all woke up to a text message from their father.  It was an image captured by a telescope near where they were in Scotland.  It showed a city in a bubble flying through the night sky.  He followed the picture with three laughing smilies.

"Can you believe they are trying to tell us this is real?" his message read.

Allen looked at the message. He recognized Atlantis, even though it wasn't a very clear picture. He wasn't surprised that someone had got a picture because there were so many satellites and telescopes now. He was surprised that the picture had been made public so quickly. He fired up his computer and searched for the picture online. It didn't take long for him to find it, and everyone was calling it fake news.

He picked the pillow and blanket up off the floor and made his bed before making his way to the kitchen where breakfast was already out. A few of the others were up as well, and they were all showing the pictures to Diana.

"I didn't even hear Diana get out of bed this morning," said Antonia. "She moves like a cat. Nani says she was down here waiting to learn how to cook."

"And she did a good job too," said Amar.

Allen realized that nobody noticed that Diana had slept in his room, and he didn't think anyone needed to know. He quickly ate some food, then grabbed Fritter and took her for a walk. It was a different world from where he had spent his last several days. There were few greetings from passersby, and everyone seemed to be in a hurry to get somewhere.

Allen was in no hurry. He knew the next adventure would find him soon.

# Other Books by Lawrence Nault

## The Draconim Series
### (YA Contemporary Eco-Fantasy)
Draconim Lacrima Mortis – Tear of the Dragon
Feeding The Fires *(Coming Soon)*

## The MacIver Kids Series *(YA Sci-Fi)*
Loma – A MacIver Kids Adventure
Diversion: A MacIver Kids Adventure

**Leviticus 25: Jubilee** *(Political/Economic Fiction)*

## The Animal Tales Series
### (Children/Early Readers)
Squirrel Tales *(e-book only)*
Wolf Tales *(e-book only)*
Bear Tales *(e-book only)*
The Mountain Hermit's Animal Tales *(The Animal Tales trilogy)*

# About The Author

Lawrence Nault, also known as The Mountain Hermit, is an author and storyteller who resides in the foothills of the Rocky Mountains. With a wealth of experience across genres, he has written books and short stories for audiences of all ages. His passion for life and learning shines through in all of his writing, whether it be about nature, animals, people, or space. His storytelling skills are evident in his work, as he deftly weaves together elements of the natural world, human emotions, and the complexities of life. In his free time, Lawrence can be found exploring the mountains, observing the animals, and taking notes for his next book. His love for nature and his surroundings has been the inspiration behind his writing, making his stories both relatable and thought-provoking.

Through every tale, whether set in a child's backyard, a distant galaxy, or a political arena, Lawrence's deep reverence for nature and the environment shines through, urging readers to reflect, respect, and act, and inspiring readers to cherish and protect our planet.

www.ingramcontent.com/pod-product-compliance
Lightning Source LLC
Chambersburg PA
CBHW071132170626
46809CB00002B/588